Crazy for You

by

Ginny Baird

Crazy for You

by

Ginny Baird

Published by

Winter Wedding Press

Copyright © 2017 Ginny Baird

Print Edition

ISBN 978-1-942058-26-7

Edited by Sally Knapp

Cover Design by Dar Albert

Chapter One

WES JOHNSON BENT down to get his morning paper at the end of his drive and an odd wailing met his ears.

"*Crazy!* Crazy, come back here!"

Wes snatched up the morning edition and stood ramrod straight as the lady across the street barreled straight at him. She wore fuzzy pink slippers and a fluttering red robe, as she darted toward Wes like a madwoman. Her long, blond hair was flying in all directions. *Well, apart from that spot near her crown holding that big hot-pink curler.* And her gaze was positively manic. Wes had heard someone new had moved into the rental across the street. No one said she'd escaped from an asylum.

"*Crazy!*" Her face contorted fiercely as she leapt at him and Wes took a giant step backwards. Something squawked at his feet, and he stared down with alarm—seeing he'd nearly stepped on a...rooster?

"I'm so sorry," the woman said, huffing and puffing. "He kind of got away."

"So I...figured."

Wes was surprised to find himself thinking the tall blonde was actually quite attractive, when she wasn't hollering at the top of her lungs. She'd clearly been captivating enough to divert Wes's attention from the encroaching bird. He hadn't even noticed it until he'd nearly flattened it with his loafer. Actually, no. He probably couldn't have done that with just one foot. The brown and white speckled animal with a towering red comb had to weigh more than twenty pounds.

The woman stooped low and scooped the complacent rooster into her arms. "You naughty boy! You could have gotten hurt!"

"Yeah," Wes said reasonably. "Including, by me."

Her pretty blue eyes lit up, as she answered breathlessly, "I know! I'm so sorry!"

Wes watched her slack-jawed, wondering when this family neighborhood had been rezoned for livestock. The answer was *never*. Surely his new neighbor knew that. Or maybe she didn't? She appeared positively out of sorts glancing around. She eyed the departing school bus rounding a faraway corner. Not five minutes ago, Wes had put his five-year-old daughter, Emma, on it. "Do you happen to know the time?" the woman asked in a mild panic.

Wes calmly checked his watch. "It's ten past seven."

"Seven?" She sucked in a gasp, and clutched the bird harder. "Oh! Oh, my! I'd better run!" She bit her bottom lip then said hurriedly, "Well, thanks for stopping Crazy!"

"Crazy?" Wes viewed her perplexedly and color warmed her cheeks. Yeah, she definitely was pretty. And young. A lot younger than Wes first gave her credit for. Not more than thirty, at most.

"That's the name of my pet." Her blush deepened as she explained further, "He showed up on my doorstep on Saturday morning."

"During that terrible storm?"

She shrugged sheepishly. "I couldn't just leave him out in the rain."

***

A flicker of amusement crossed his handsome face, and Mary Ellen's heart pounded. *What* had she been thinking, bringing that wayward chicken into her house? It had been a far-flung idea. Ludicrous! Something that had occurred to her in the *weakest of weak* moments. She'd glanced up and down the empty street, then into the rooster's sad dark eyes. He'd looked precisely like she'd felt. Defeated. Downcast... And, utterly alone. He'd also appeared rather like a drowned rat, only a bit larger and with soaking white feathers.

Mary Ellen's heart immediately went out to the pitiful looking creature. At the same time, he seemed concerned for her. It was if he could intuitively tell that Mary Ellen was badly in need of a friend. As she'd only been in Paradise, Virginia a few days, she hadn't exactly had the chance to meet anybody... Until now!

Mary Ellen realized with a jolt that her first potential introduction stood staring her in the eyes. His eyes were a verdant meadow green, too. Lush and inviting. *Stop it, Mary Ellen!* she scolded herself firmly. *This gorgeous dark-haired guy is surely married!*

She spotted the small pink bicycle with training wheels through the open garage door at his back, and her suspicions were confirmed. Of course, he was taken. All the cute ones typically were. This was probably why no adorable kittens had landed on her stoop, and she'd been saddled with a humongous chicken instead.

She shifted Crazy in her arms and jutted out her hand. "I'm Mary Ellen. Nice to meet you."

He gave a slow curious grin and a dimple settled in his right cheek. "Wes." He took her hand and Mary Ellen's heart fluttered. Not good at all. She had to get away from this very married man. "Welcome to Sweetheart Valley Hills," he said, referencing the name of the neighborhood.

Mary Ellen's hand shot to the top of her head when she saw him goggling that way. *Argh.* She'd *totally* forgotten about that roller! If she didn't wear it to bed, her hair developed a cowlick, sticking straight up near her center part. Sort of like... She briefly glanced at the bird she held.

"So you named your rooster Crazy?" Wes asked, interrupting her thoughts.

She hadn't done it immediately. She'd decided on the name during his arduous first night at home, during which she'd realized roosters can make an awful lot of noise when provoked.

Apparently, being cooped up in the laundry room was provoking. He'd completely clawed up the door and left untidy animal droppings all over the dryer. Mary Ellen found a place near the edge of town that sold wire cages and chicken feed by searching online, and had raced out to purchase more suitable supplies the next morning.

She stealthily eyed her pet, noting he was being suspiciously quiet. Probably dreaming up something crafty to do. He'd stolen several pieces of her jewelry already, and had made an utter wreck of her house. Which was why he was staying penned up today while she was away.

"Um, yeah," she said, her teeth gritted just slightly. "I know it sounds a little weird."

"Not any crazier than having a chicken for a pet." He grinned and Mary Ellen's heart hammered harder. Okay, this was it. She absolutely had to go. She and men were a bad combination these days. She'd just traveled clear across the state to forget about one of them.

Clean air, bucolic surrounding countryside! With scenic Blue Ridge Mountain views and a charming downtown area. The Chamber of Commerce materials had made the historic town of Paradise, Virginia sound really intriguing, until she'd actually arrived here and realized she didn't know a soul in town. Hence, Mary Ellen's foolhardy acceptance of her fine-feathered houseguest.

She'd tried phoning the SPCA before going to the Horse and Hay Feed and Seed, but no local farmers had reported a rooster missing. As best the volunteer answering the phone could guess, Crazy might have fallen off a chicken truck a few days before. There'd been a minor fender bender on the bypass, and a handful of foul had escaped. When Mary Ellen asked where the truck had been going, the fellow answered, "Lady, you don't want to know."

He further said that if she'd found one of the birds, she might as well hang onto him. She could either do that, or bring Crazy to the shelter, where the rooster could take his chances in finding a new adoptive home—or not. *Chickens are very loving, you know*, the shelter worker had told her leadingly. *Yours will likely have a much longer life expectancy with you, than in the place where he was headed...*

She'd hung up the phone and tossed the half-price oven roaster chicken she'd bought on sale directly in the freezer with a pang of guilt. Who knew if she'd ever eat poultry again?

"I'd love to stay and chat," she told Wes, stepping sideways. Luckily this was a quiet street and they lived on a cul-de-sac, so no cars were coming. "But I've got to get to work!"

"Yeah, me too." He perused her oddly, quietly assessing her. "Well, Mary Ellen..." He tipped his rolled-up paper in a salute. "Have a good day!"

She inched toward the curb, nearly stumbling off it. "Yeah! You, too!"

Then, she clutched Crazy to her chest and scurried back across the street, mortification seeping through her. Hopefully things would go better at her new job! The day surely couldn't get any more humiliating than this. Oh yeah, it could, she thought as she tripped out of one of her slippers. The icy cold grass met her toes, snaking between them. It was mid-October and the lawn was frosty, a fine morning mist masking the air.

Mary Ellen tightened her grip on Crazy and quickly nabbed her slipper, brandishing it at Wes in a wave. Then she scuttled toward her house in a hop-skipping motion that caused Crazy to blink up at her. "Don't say a word," she hissed softly. "Not one little peep."

***

Wes sat as his desk in the principal's office at Turtle Creek Elementary, going over his secretary's notes. He'd only been gone two weeks, but they had been eventful ones. His daughter's kindergarten teacher had experienced some sort of public meltdown in front of the class. She'd sobbed that she still loved her ex-husband and was going back to him, "in spite of what he's done"...and had to be dragged from the room—in a fit of hysteria—by her teaching assistant. The outburst had supposedly been inspired by the class voting to name their new pair of guinea pigs Romeo and Juliet. The TA had unwittingly suggested it, and no one had been able to reach Ms. Cantor since. She'd left a resignation note in the secretary's mailbox the next morning and bolted for somewhere over the Blue Ridge Mountains.

The stack of phone messages Wes had to answer from troubled parents was enormous. At least, he'd have good news to share about a suitable replacement when he returned the calls. Fortunately, the school secretary, Becky, had been able to line up an experienced substitute, while Central Office moved quickly to fill the unexpected vacancy. They had a few candidates in mind who'd applied to the district after the start of the year. Upon completing virtual interviews with their optimal long-distance candidates, they'd found the perfect match. Someone with good credentials who appeared very level headed.

Miss Meeks was a younger teacher, but she came highly recommended by her previous school. After three satisfactory years on the job, she'd taken a few months off to care for her sickly mother. Talented, stable, responsible, with obviously solid family values. This candidate sounded ideal. Wes hadn't had time to peruse her folder, but he'd take a quick look now. The new teacher was due in at any minute to complete her paperwork, receive a tour of the school, and meet her kindergarten class. She'd begin teaching tomorrow.

Wes ran a hand through his hair, thinking the timing of this classroom catastrophe couldn't have been worse. He wished he'd been here personally to be involved in the hiring process, but he trusted Central Office to have made a good pick. It wasn't like Wes could have prevented his absence anyway. He and Emma had been on the West Coast for the sad occasion of Emma's grandma's passing. First, the little girl had lost her mother, and now the maternal grandparent she held so dear. The loss had hit Wes hard as well.

His late mother-in-law, Carol, was the last bit of Patricia's family he had left. Carol's husband, Derek, had died years before, not too long after Wes and Patricia's wedding. Derek had never known his granddaughter, Emma. And, the little girl had only been blessed with a few short years of knowing her mother, before Patricia succumbed to cancer.

That had been two and a half years ago, and Emma's vague memories of her mom were fading already. Naturally, Emma hadn't been old enough to remember much, but she did claim to recall Patricia's lovely singing voice. Wes sometimes thought he still heard it...through Emma's open bedroom window, late in the evening after Emma had been tucked into bed and he sat on his front porch alone. But Wes understood that was all in his head, and in his very lonely heart.

Someone knocked at his door and Wes stared at the folder in his hands, realizing he hadn't even cracked it open. He'd been so lost in his reverie about Patricia, and her mom's recent funeral, he'd totally lost track of the time. He swallowed hard past the lump in his throat, gathering his resolve. He was at work, for crying out loud. Not to mention *the principal.* He had no business bringing his personal worries here.

Wes straightened his pumpkin-patterned tie over the button-down shirt he wore beneath his tweed jacket. He then called loudly, "Come in!"

Becky slowly opened the door, and Wes gawked at the apparition. It couldn't be, but it was! His nutty chicken-chasing neighbor from across the street.

Chapter Two

MARY ELLEN STARED through the open doorway into the principal's office, and the blood drained from her face the instant she recognized her handsome neighbor. *Okay, it's official. This is absolutely the worst day of my life! All right, maybe not "the worst" day...* That had come when Jeff left her, saying he wanted somebody more interesting and assertive in his life. Gee, like that aggressive, mad-dog attorney new girlfriend of his that Mary Ellen had seen on Jeff's Facebook? Mary Ellen was interesting! Just look at all the daring choices she'd made! She was also quite assertive. Sort of. Particularly when she wasn't around her domineering mother.

She felt a tad lightheaded as the plump middle-aged secretary presented her. Becky had short, layered brown hair with gold highlights and a kindly face offset by alert dark eyes that shone like copper pennies. She wore a charcoal shell with a matching cardigan sweater over black polyester slacks. Each of her earrings looked like a miniature chalkboard eraser, and her necklace sported an array of colorful wooden crayons draped from her neck in a cheerful semicircle.

"Mr. Johnson," Becky said, addressing the stunned-looking man behind the desk. "Miss Meeks is here to sign her forms and meet her class."

Wes stood to greet her. "Of course." He extended his hand and Mary Ellen walked forward on wobbly knees to shake it. "Good to see you." His eyes roved over her in a curious way, and for an instant Mary Ellen hoped he wouldn't identify her as that crazy chicken-chasing woman from Sweetheart Valley Hills. She did look pretty different dressed and with her makeup on. "*Again*," he added, and Mary Ellen's grin tightened.

"What a small world!" she exclaimed, her voice rising. Then she quickly explained to the secretary, who was observing them with interest, "Mr. Johnson and I live right across the street from each other. We met just this morning."

"Yes," Wes said, deadpan. "In a *crazy* kind of way." His green eyes twinkled, and Mary Ellen suspected he was teasing her. He clearly couldn't be flirting. That would be unprofessional, and Wes didn't seem like the type of man who'd make that kind of gaff. He appeared to be the upright sort. Principled and controlled. Fully in charge of his demeanor and emotions.

"Please, have a seat." He indicated a chair facing his desk and Mary Ellen took it, as Becky backed away. Mary Ellen self-consciously crossed her legs, adjusting the hemline of her tasteful, khaki-colored shirtwaist dress at her knees. She'd donned sensible chestnut-colored flats and carried a matching leather bag, which she set on the floor beside her.

"Coffee?" Becky asked with a congenial smile.

"Coffee would be great, thanks," Mary Ellen returned pleasantly. "I take mine black."

"Make that two," Wes petitioned warmly as he took his own chair.

After the secretary left, Wes met Mary Ellen's gaze. "Well, Miss Meeks," he said, drumming his fingers against the personnel file on his desk. "It is a small world, indeed."

"About this morning—" Mary Ellen began in a rush.

Wes waved his hand. "Already forgotten. That is..." He paused to study her and Mary Ellen's heart hammered. "Unless you're planning on bringing your rooster to school?"

"Crazy?" She quickly pressed her lips together, then responded more calmly. "No, no. I wouldn't dream of it."

"The class already has two pets," Wes continued lightly. "A couple of guinea pigs named Romeo and Juliet."

Mary Ellen tried not to blush at the hint of romance. So what if the class pair was named for Shakespeare's ill-fated duo? That had nothing to do with her job, or why she was sitting here. "I like guinea pigs," she stated confidentially. "My class cared for several at my last school."

"Several?" Wes's brow rose with the question and Mary Ellen held her breath, wondering whether or not she should mention the body count.

"I taught for three years!" she filled in as if that explained it. Which it did, naturally. In part. How was she to know that tomato leaves were deadly to guinea pigs? If she'd been aware of that fact, Mary Ellen clearly wouldn't have placed her students' fledgling potted plant projects on the windowsill beside the guinea pig cage.

"Yes," Wes said, cracking open her file. "That was in...Hopewell, Virginia?" He glanced up and Mary Ellen fell into his field-green gaze. Elementary school principal or not, Wes was undeniably handsome. With his solid, buff frame and those big broad shoulders, he looked more like a firefighter than an administrator. The strong and capable sort, who effortlessly carried screaming women from burning buildings. Mary Ellen tried not to mentally reprise the image of herself storming across the street wearing her fluttering robe and gigantic curler.

Instead, she worked really, really hard to focus on that bicycle.

"I'm sorry?" Wes asked perplexedly. "Did you just say something about training wheels?"

"I...er...did I?" Mary Ellen's cheeks flamed. "What I meant was, that's where I got my training! Teacher training in Hopewell! I did my student teaching there before moving to—"

"Ah yes, sorry. I see." His eyes were back on her resume. "Surry County. Is that near Williamsburg?"

"Just across the James River, yes."

"Nice area."

"You know it?"

"I took Emma to the Historic Triangle once. Jamestown, Williamsburg, and Yorktown. It was during one of her grandma's visits to the East Coast."

"Where does Emma's grandmother live?" Mary Ellen asked, making conversation. This was good. Better than good. Mary Ellen could draw Wes out about his family, so he'd believe her politely interested. Which might cause him to doubt the fact that Mary Ellen had been ogling him previously. Which she hadn't done, of course. Not intentionally, anyway. And you could hardly consider that her fault. Wes had no business being her boss and looking the way he did...which was...*flaming...hot.*

Mary Ellen absently glanced around the room, then grabbed an after-school program brochure from a nearby table and used it to fan herself.

"She and her late husband lived in Seattle," Wes continued, answering her earlier question about his daughter's grandmother. "Both are deceased now."

"Oh, gosh. I'm sorry."

Wes viewed her curiously and Mary Ellen's arm stopped flapping. "Are you warm, Miss Meeks?" Mary Ellen gripped the end of the brochure until it crinkled.

"Not really!" she cried, as perspiration swept her hairline.

Wes watched her steadily as she set the offending flyer down, patting it twice for good measure once she'd placed it back on the table beside her chair. "And, um...please! Call me Mary Ellen."

"Only if you'll call me Wes." He surprised her with a smile and a tiny droplet of sweat broke free, dribbling down her left temple. Mary Ellen quickly smoothed back her hair, unobtrusively wiping the moisture away.

"Wes, sure! No problem."

"But only when there are no students around. Or parents," he added, after a thought.

Mary Ellen knew the protocol well, because it had been much the same at her past two schools. "I certainly understand."

Wes gently closed her folder and set his elbows on his desk, catching her off guard with a new topic of conversation. "I have to tell you, Mary Ellen," he said with sincere green eyes. "Even though this may not relate directly to your teaching credentials, on a personal and truly heartfelt note... I was very impressed with how you handled your mother's situation."

Mother? Mary Ellen wasn't sure what her mother had to do with anything? She racked her brain for an explanation, wondering if this had to do with that rumor...

"How is your mom, by the way?" Wes's expression registered genuine concern. "Doing somewhat better, I hope?"

"I...er...well..."

"I want you to understand that I'm not merely speaking as your boss, here. We at Turtle Creek Elementary are all like family. We like to think we understand and support employees with core values like yours. Because, frankly, those are our values, too."

Mary Ellen stalled for time, trying to think of something to say. In truth, it had been an enormous misunderstanding. By the time Jeff dumped her, she'd already resigned from her job at her old school and been replaced by another teacher. Her mom, Liz, had insisted on helping Mary Ellen mend her broken heart by taking her to a healing spa in New Mexico. Somehow the word got out among Mary Ellen's former colleagues that Liz was the one ailing—and in need of her daughter's support.

The rumor mill spun it so Jeff hadn't even been an issue at all. The idea of Mary Ellen moving to Boston to marry her boyfriend had all been a "cover story" designed to veil the truth about Mary Ellen's dire family situation, wherein Mary Ellen needed to relocate to Washington, DC to care for her incredibly disabled mother.

Mary Ellen *had* actually moved to DC—at her mom's behest, but mostly because she needed to get her head together. Since she'd already decided on leaving Virginia anyway, Mary Ellen hadn't bothered to correct any misperceptions among her former coworkers before she departed. Mostly, because it truly wasn't any of their business. She'd never even remotely imagined the unfounded rumor of her mother's illness would somehow make it into her personnel file!

Wes eyed her with compassion, mistaking her silence for deeper worry about her mom. "I apologize for bringing up something so personal," he said kindly. "I'd merely hoped, since you'd returned to work, that meant her situation was improving?"

Liz's circumstances were continually improving. Apart from holding a high-ranking position at a Washington think tank, she'd won the ladies' tennis championship at her exclusive country club for the sixth straight year. "Liz, she's..." Mary Ellen's pulse quickened as she struggled to answer. "Doing just fine. But, how did you—?"

"Your last principal, Mr. Fuller, was very clear in praising you in his glowing letter of recommendation," Wes explained. "Buddy Jenkins from Central Office told me all about it when he phoned first thing this morning to explain why you'd overwhelmingly been selected as our new hire.

"There's obviously no mention of your mother's ill health in your work records, but Mr. Fuller did make a point of underscoring your incredibly admirable reason for temporarily dropping out of the workforce. Normally, a teacher taking leave at the start of the year would be seen in an unfavorable light. However, given your very unusual circumstances and extremely worthy motives, we in the Sweetheart Valley School District certainly understand."

Worthy? Mary Ellen wasn't so sure the tortured poetry she'd written would qualify as such. Thank goodness, she'd destroyed every line of it before she'd left DC. As her five-year teaching license was still valid, it hadn't even occurred to her that the short career hiatus would be an issue. And, if anyone had cared to ask, she'd been prepared to say she'd simply needed a brief break for personal reasons.

Perhaps she should take pains to clear the matter up now, rather than let Wes's false impression linger. "Wes, about my time off—"

"Two cups of coffee! Nice and hot," Becky announced from the doorway, briskly striding forward. She handed one steaming paper cup to Mary Ellen and set the other down on Wes's desk. "If you're taking Miss Meeks to meet the children, now might be a good time," she informed him. "Ms. Cantor's class breaks for recess in precisely five minutes."

"Thanks, Becky," Wes said with a nod before returning his gaze to Mary Ellen. After the secretary left, he prodded, "You were saying?"

"Oh, I just...don't want you to get the wrong impression. About my mother. It's not that she really... What I mean is, I didn't so much..."

"No need for false modesty..." Wes's eyes twinkled as he sipped from his cup. "You did the right thing—the *caring* thing—in putting family first. The fact that you took time off to tend to your mom demonstrates your strength of character." He chuckled good-naturedly. "It's not like you were off 'finding yourself'—while writing dark poetry, or something," he said, clearly joking. "Ha-ha!"

"Ha-ha!" Mary Ellen echoed with fake cheer. "Nope! Not me!"

Wes took another quick sip of coffee and checked his watch. "We should probably go greet the class, then Becky can give you the full tour of the school. You'll have some forms to complete. But, don't worry. Becky's very, very good with details. If you have any questions, she'll help you. She's been at the school since I was a student here, and she totally knows the ropes."

"You went to Turtle Creek Elementary? That's incredible."

Wes's eyes sparkled as he stood, motioning for Mary Ellen to join him. "Now, my daughter's here too. I guess you could say it's somewhat of a family tradition."

Chapter Three

MARY ELLEN LOOKED down at the gaggle of kindergarten children and twenty-two cherubic faces stared back at her. They were sitting on a large rectangular rug by a nest of stocked bookshelves. The substitute teacher sitting in the rocking chair in front of them smiled pleasantly at Mary Ellen and Wes, who stood beside her.

"Class," the substitute said, closing the book that she'd been reading. "It appears we have some visitors this morning."

Wes nodded cordially and clasped his hands together in front of him, grinning broadly. "Good morning, children."

"Good morning, Mr. Johnson," they replied in unison. Mary Ellen loved the sound of their little voices, so hopeful and trusting. She would do her best to be a good teacher to them. While Mary Ellen didn't know the specifics of the situation, she'd gathered that their previous teacher had left rather abruptly, and without giving the school much warning.

She glanced around the room, seeing that the walls were decorated in the children's artwork. One series of paintings showcased trees sprouting leaves fashioned from the children's handprints in fall colors: reds, golds, oranges, and browns. Observing the creative project, Mary Ellen understood her predecessor must have been accomplished at her job. It was a shame that she'd left so early in the year, disappointing the children in her class. Then again, Ms. Cantor's departure had provided Mary Ellen with her opening.

Wes had been speaking for a few moments, introducing her and saying she'd start being their new teacher in the morning. This announcement was greeted by tiny gasps of joy and *yippee*s, causing the edges of the substitute's mouth to droop just a little.

"I know you'll all miss Mrs. Taylor," Wes said, empathetically picking up on the substitute's stance. "She's done a fine job here, hasn't she?"

The kids all nodded compliantly with big wide eyes, which suddenly turned on Mary Ellen. She smiled sweetly at the group. "It's so great to be here and meet you. Like Mr. Johnson said, I'm Miss Meeks. Why don't you start by telling me *your* names?" When they beamed up at her, she added, "I'm sure I'll learn much more about you tomorrow."

Just then, a slight woman with short spiky black-and-purple hair, who appeared to be close to forty, entered the room. She wore a craft apron and a school ID badge, identifying her as a teaching assistant. Mary Ellen guessed she was the one assigned to this room. Wes drew a finger to his lips and the newcomer nodded in understanding, not wanting to interrupt Mary Ellen's meet and greet with the kids.

A wiry little boy with a cocoa-colored complexion and big brown eyes was the first to chime in. "I'm Bobby!"

"I'm Eliza!" announced a blue-eyed girl in pigtails.

"My name's Wilson!" a boy with red hair and freckles shouted at the top of his lungs.

"One at a time, please. One at a time." Mr. Johnson calmly raised a hand while Mary Ellen stifled a chuckle. "And you know the rule..." His gaze roved over them, and the children sat at attention, several of their hands shooting up.

"That's better." Mary Ellen nodded with approval. She went around the group calling on the kids in turn. All were absolutely precious, but she could already tell who the energetic ones were. Mary Ellen couldn't wait to get started channeling their energy in the right direction. Working with high-octane kids was one of her strong suits. Yet, there was one child in the group who didn't seem quite as exuberant. She wore a plaid dress with tights, and had long brown hair parted in the middle with both top sections pulled back in barrettes.

"And what's your name?" Mary Ellen asked kindly. For some reason she sensed Wes watching the exchange with special interest.

The child turned her forest-green gaze on Mary Ellen, and Mary Ellen felt a spark of familiarity. Wes had said his daughter attended Turtle Creek Elementary. Could this little girl be his? By the warm way he watched her, Mary Ellen suspected that perhaps she was.

"I'm Emma," the little girl said. She pointed shyly to Wes. "And he's my daddy."

The other children giggled. "He's the prince!" Wilson informed Mary Ellen knowledgeably. More cackles erupted, particularly from Bobby, who was clutching his belly and rolling sideways onto the carpet.

"Principal!" Bobby cried, rollicking.

Wes gently quieted them with a downward motion of his palms. "Thank you for clearing that up, Bobby. Now, let's all please remember our manners."

Emma's gaze was still locked on Mary Ellen. After a beat, she asked softly, "Are you going to run away and get married?"

Mary Ellen's face flamed. "Er...no." She cast a sideways glance at Wes and her color deepened. "I'm sure that I won't. Not any time soon."

"My mommy says marriage sometimes doesn't last," Eliza commented without prompting. "That's why she and Daddy divorced."

Mary Ellen gazed sympathetically at the girl, then a pretty girl with dark bangs shouted, "My mommy's Japanese!"

A child with plaits and rosy cheeks called out, "*My* mommy and daddy are Mexican!"

Wes coughed pointedly and the kids pursed their lips and sat at attention. "I think that will be all for today. You'll have plenty of time to speak to Miss Meeks tomorrow." He gave them each a cautionary perusal, his gaze lingering a few seconds longer on Wilson and Bobby. "I expect you'll all behave and make Miss Meeks feel welcome?"

The children nodded enthusiastically, and Mary Ellen smiled at the group.

"I can't wait to get started."

***

While the substitute led the children outdoors to recess, Wes introduced Mary Ellen to her teaching assistant, Tina Miller. He left them chatting for a moment, excusing himself as he had a parent meeting. He'd asked Mary Ellen to return to the front office when she was done speaking with Tina, so Becky could show her the rest of the school. She could also complete her paperwork then. She'd agreed happily and thanked him for his warm welcome.

Warm was right. Holy cow. What was wrong with him? Wes was broiling under his jacket. All he'd done was shake Mary Ellen's hand, saying he looked forward to seeing her tomorrow, and—totally without warning—his blood had started pumping harder. Wes loosened his tie, thinking this wasn't good. Not good at all. He wasn't supposed to become attracted to his teachers. Nothing like that had ever happened to him before. Wes was very skilled at keeping his professional distance. Mostly, because that had come easy.

Though Patricia had been gone for more than two years, sometimes it seemed like her passing had occurred only yesterday. In many ways, Wes still felt like a married man. Isn't that why he still wore his wedding band?

Wes glanced guiltily at the shiny gold ring on his left hand, recalling his sister's prodding that he remove it. Jenny was six years younger than him, but awfully bossy for a baby sister. She ran the ice cream shop in town, Cherry on Top. While Emma loved going there for ice cream, lately, Wes had slacked off on taking her. It seemed every cone didn't just come with the requisite whipped cream, sprinkles, and maraschino cherry; it was also delivered with a hearty dose of unsolicited advice. Jenny was convinced that Wes had mourned Patricia's passing for long enough, and that he needed to *get on with his life*. Both for his sake, and Emma's. *How are you ever going to meet a woman, bro, if you keep thinking and acting like you're married?*

Well, maybe Wes wasn't ready to meet another woman. Replacing Patricia wasn't just unimaginable. It seemed impossible. The two of them had met in college in California, and they'd quickly fallen in love. Wes had been in a five-year program that culminated with him receiving his masters in teaching, and Patricia had majored in music. They'd married shortly after graduation then relocated to Wes's hometown of Paradise, Virginia, where he'd been offered a teaching position at Turtle Creek Elementary. Patricia took a job at a local card store, which she eventually came to manage. And, together, they'd bought their first home.

Wes attended evening classes to obtain his doctorate in education, and after he completed his degree, he and Patricia had Emma. The day Wes was promoted to principal was the day that they received Patricia's devastating diagnosis. No professional transition could have felt as bittersweet. By the time Wes officially assumed his new post, his wife was already very ill. She was gone by the spring of his first administrative year. It had been a tough blow to him and considerably confusing for Emma, who called for her mommy and couldn't grasp where her loving mother had gone.

It had been a heartbreaking time, and one that Wes had believed he'd never get over. Until...he'd seen Mary Ellen barreling at him chasing her rooster, with that crazed look on her face. Something about his new neighbor had unhinged him, in a truly unusual way. Maybe it had been the element of surprise, or that panic-stricken look in her pretty blue eyes. And they *were* pretty, too. Wes couldn't very well deny it. And, it wasn't just about Mary Ellen's eyes. She was pretty all over. With that totally sweet face and that beautiful blond hair, and her fit, athletic figure. Wes stopped walking to pull a handkerchief from his pocket and mop his brow.

He had to cut it out. He couldn't do this. Mary Ellen was much more than his hot new neighbor. She was his employee, for goodness' sakes. Being as kind and gifted as she apparently was, she also likely had a boyfriend waiting in the wings somewhere. Somebody who was desperately missing her and primed to visit her in Paradise, the moment Mary Ellen gave him the go-ahead.

Wes straightened his lapels and approached his office door. Two sets of parents sat waiting in opposing chairs wearing scowls on their faces. Becky apparently had brought in extra chairs for the couples, who'd arrived to discuss their fifth grade sons' lunchtime assault on the cafeteria by inducing a food fight. Wes steeled himself for a long meeting and stepped through his office door. Then he carefully closed it behind him.

Chapter Four

LATER THAT AFTERNOON, Mary Ellen sat at her kitchen table going over her to-do list as Crazy fluttered in his cage in the corner. "Just another few minutes," she told him. "Then I'll take you out for your walk." Mary Ellen understood that her pet needed exercise, but she didn't exactly trust him turned loose in the house anymore. Apart from absconding with her things, the rooster had nearly damaged *himself* by trying to fly right through the sliding glass door to the back patio. Mary Ellen had thought that having a fenced backyard would help in keeping her animal contained, but she supposed that only worked with dogs. Small dogs, and not the jumping-over-the-fence kind.

Crazy was definitely the jumping-over-the-fence kind of chicken. Hadn't he demonstrated that this morning? Her face steamed as she recalled her impromptu early meeting with Wes. At least he'd seemed to take the encounter in good humor, and didn't appear to hold her chicken-chasing episode against her. What a sight she must have been!

"You didn't start your week off very well," she said, looking askance at the bird.

Crazy clawed at the base of his cage and made an undignified squawk. This rooster was seriously demanding. She'd already fed him twice since coming home, and had provided several bowls of fresh water—which he kept turning over in an apparent attempt to vex her.

Right. *Buy bird water bottle.* She added that to her list, thinking she'd seen those devices for parakeets. Surely, they made something similar for chickens? At the very least she could purchase one of those pressure-activated upside-down water jugs with a pet dish underneath. Mary Ellen couldn't have Crazy going thirsty, but she was genuinely tired of mopping the kitchen floor. Each time he upended his bowl, water cascaded out of his wire cage and went sloshing everywhere.

Crazy's cage stood about two feet tall and was three feet across and deep. When she'd purchased it, Mary Ellen had also bought what she thought was a two-week supply of chicken feed. Given Crazy's rabid appetite, Mary Ellen wasn't sure it would last that long. For a brief moment, she wondered if she shouldn't have named her pet "Mr. Piggy." This last thought made her giggle, capturing the bird's attention.

He stared at her with intelligent dark eyes, as if waiting on her to do something. Yeah, and she knew what. "All right," Mary Ellen said with a sigh. "I'll take you outdoors. But this time, please. *Behave.*"

***

Mary Ellen opened the sliding glass door and carried Crazy outside. Her rental was a ranch-style home with three bedrooms and two baths. It was plenty large enough and provided both an office for her and a guest room for folks to come visit. No one she knew had planned to come out so far. Apart from her mother, who'd threatened to descend on her at the first opportunity. Mary Ellen loved her mom, she really did. Liz was accomplished, generous, and extremely successful. She was also terribly pushy, and one hundred percent certain about what was best for her daughter. And that was *not* being a teacher. Liz wanted Mary Ellen to explore her creative side. Mary Ellen had. *And failed.* Failed at being a dancer... *What a disaster!*

Failed at writing fiction. *Ugh.* Failed in her fledgling musical career. *Hoo-boy.* Mary Ellen buried her face in her hands, temporarily losing sight of Crazy. Oh right! There he was... Pecking contentedly at the grass near the edge of the patio.

Mary Ellen scuttled in his direction, attempting to keep him corralled with her feet as he meandered around. He didn't appear to be making any attempts at a getaway, so Mary Ellen relaxed just a little, her thoughts still focused on her mother, who Mary Ellen suspected was trying to live vicariously through her. Liz had gone into finance, but had secretly wanted to be a painter. This made her believe that Mary Ellen had hidden creative ambitions as well. Mary Ellen was creative! She funneled tons of creativity into her teaching, but somehow her mom couldn't make a connection with that.

When Mary Ellen had moved in with her mom after resigning from her last teaching position, Liz had seized on the opportunity to steer Mary Ellen in the "right" direction. Didn't the timing of this recent misfortune prove that teaching wasn't for her? Mary Ellen finally had a chance to break free and be daring! And, Liz would do everything in her power to support her. Yeah, like practically locking Mary Ellen in her room until she'd completed that entire volume of really awful poetry. In the leather notebook with a hand-stitched binding that Liz had given her along with a set of extremely elegant designer pens. It didn't help that Mary Ellen's work was maudlin and entirely focused on a broken-hearted protagonist. *Poem after poem...after poem...after poem...after poem...* The vast majority of them didn't even rhyme!

It didn't take long for Mary Ellen to decide that she was ready to stand on her own two feet—again, and as soon as humanly possible—before her mom drove her totally nuts. Mary Ellen fired up her laptop and began applying to teaching positions all over Virginia. The farther away she could get from DC and the Tidewater area the better. The Sweetheart Valley town called Paradise, in the foothills of the Blue Ridge Mountains, looked ideal.

Mary Ellen startled at a squawking sound, searching the yard. *Crazy!* Where had he gone? She heard the roar of a school bus dragging to a halt on the street just as she spied Crazy's flicking tail feathers disappearing over the top of the fence.

***

The moment the afternoon school bus pulled away, Wes had an uncanny sense of déjà vu.

"Daddy, look!" Emma cried pointing. "It's Miss Meeks with a chicken!"

It was actually more like Miss Meeks in hot pursuit of her rooster!

"Crazy! No!" She darted across the road, as Crazy scurried along with outstretched wings. Wes wondered where on earth the bird was going, but he soon saw that Crazy was headed straight for him and Emma. Crazy waddled wildly toward them, and Wes stepped protectively in front of his daughter. At that exact second, the bird paused at Wes's feet and lowered his wings.

"I'm so sorry!" Mary Ellen called, catching up with her runaway pet. Her cheeks burned brightly as she met Wes's eyes. "Again."

Emma peered around her daddy's legs. "You're my new teacher."

"Yes. Yes, that's right." Mary Ellen smiled tightly and reached for her bird, scooping him into her arms. "Hello, Emma."

"Hello," the child said, and then her brow knitted. "Is that your pet?"

Mary Ellen shifted the rooster in her arms. "He is! His name is..." She hesitated a beat. "Crazy."

Emma giggled into her hand. "That's a silly name."

Mary Ellen shrugged in agreement, avoiding Wes's gaze. "I know."

"He seems to like to stretch his wings," Wes said wryly. "That's twice in one day."

"I don't know how he got away! I was watching so carefully!"

"Watching?" Wes viewed Mary Ellen with amusement, surmising she was a city girl who'd taken on a country-sized problem. "You mean, you don't have a coop?"

"Coop?" she asked, like he'd spoken in a foreign language.

"A chicken coop," Wes went on to explain. "You know, the sort made from *chicken* wire."

"Oh, right. Right!" She blinked in understanding, appearing mildly befuddled. "No, sorry. Haven't got one."

"Well then, that could be your trouble."

"Chickens can fly over fences," Emma observed sagely.

"Yes. Yes, I learned that," Mary Ellen confided, embarrassed to know less that a five-year-old. She hoped this information wouldn't sour Wes on her as being Emma's teacher. Mary Ellen had tons of great smarts in other ways!

"You can probably find supplies at the hardware store."

The color drained from her face. "Supplies?" she asked weakly. "You mean, I have to build it?"

Wes viewed her astutely. "Something tells me you don't know your way around a hammer."

"Sure I do!" she protested quickly. "It's got two ends! The handle, and the...the..."

"Head," Emma said, grinning.

"Right! I knew that!"

Wes slowly shook his head. "Where do you keep Crazy now?"

"In a cage in the kitchen." Mary Ellen gave an embarrassed flush. "I didn't even think about a coop, truthfully. I've been so busy settling in. I only moved here last—"

"And yet," Wes said, smiling at her. "You adopted a rooster?"

"I was lone—" She stopped herself, swallowing hard. "I mean, *he* was. Crazy. Not saying that 'he was Crazy'... What I meant was..."

Wes gave a low chuckle, utterly charmed by her. "No worries. I get it."

Mary Ellen nervously skittered backwards. "Well, anyway. Thanks for the tip! I think you're right. A coop might be the solution. I'll get right on it. Right...right away." She glanced at the little girl wearing her school backpack. "Nice seeing you, Emma! I'm excited for our first day tomorrow!"

Before she turned away, Wes said, "I can help you if you'd like."

Mary Ellen's jaw dropped open but there was gratitude in her sweet blue eyes. "You...you'd do that?"

"Daddy's good with a hammer," Emma informed her. "He built my doll house."

"Oh! Oh, how sweet." She appeared to ponder his proposition. "That's really kind of you to offer," she said to Wes. "But I'd hate to take you away from your other..." She briefly studied the child. "Family business."

"Emma can help." He affectionately eyed his daughter, who'd been assisting him with handyman type projects for the past year. "Can't you, Emma?"

"Uh-huh!" She gave a toothy grin that showed her two central incisors were missing.

Mary Ellen studied them uncertainly. "Are you sure your wife—"

"Patricia's been gone for a while now," Wes said, and the information clearly stunned her. Mary Ellen's gaze darted to his left hand then she rapidly looked away.

"Oh my." Mary Ellen shared a worried look. "I'm so sorry for you both."

"It's all right," Emma chimed in. "Mommy's in heaven with the angels. Grandma and Grandpa are too."

Mary Ellen's face fell. "I'm sure that's hard." She observed the pair sympathetically. "For both of you."

"We have Grammy and Poppy!" Emma proclaimed brightly. "Aunt Jenny, too!"

Wes smiled warmly at his daughter before addressing Mary Ellen. "We're lucky to have family in town. My folks live nearby and my sister Jenny runs the ice cream shop, Cherry on Top."

"Boy-oh-boy, Daddy! Can we go for ice cream?" Emma tugged at Wes's hand. "With Miss Meeks?"

Heat warmed the back of his neck. "Well, I don't know when—"

"How about after we build the coop?" Emma asked. She grinned brightly. "On Saturday?"

Wes watched his daughter perplexedly and she folded her little arms. "That's when we always do our projects," she told Mary Ellen. "Week days are for homework," she said sternly, imitating her father. "Work before play!"

Mary Ellen stared at them blankly, clearly unsure of what to say. She turned undecidedly toward Wes, who felt caught out.

"I don't see any reason we can't get ice cream—after the work is done."

"Only if I pay," Mary Ellen insisted, as Crazy wriggled in her arms. "It's the least I can do for your...help."

"All right, then. It's settled." Wes clapped his hands together, wondering what he'd just signed on for. Certainly not a date. *No, no.* Not that. Dating his brand new hire would *not* be cool.

"Yay!" Emma yelped with glee and Wes's heart stuttered. He was just being helpful. Absolutely! Playing the part of the good neighbor. That's all this was.

"Maybe if you give me a list or something before then," Mary Ellen suggested. "I can purchase any supplies we'll need?"

Wes wasn't certain he trusted the woman who couldn't identify both ends of a hammer to pick out lumber. "Why don't you leave that to me?" he responded gallantly.

"Fine. Then we'll settle up later."

"Sure," Wes agreed. Though, privately, he didn't intend to charge Mary Ellen a thing. Once it was complete, he'd ask her to consider the chicken coop his and Emma's housewarming gift. Apart from being their new neighbor, she was also his daughter's teacher, and—especially given her current predicament with Crazy—Mary Ellen would surely prefer a chicken coop to a shiny red apple.

Chapter Five

MARY ELLEN PULLED into the school parking lot the next morning a ball of nerves. She wasn't anxious about facing her class. The children were adorable and she was confident in her ability to handle them, even the energetic ones. She'd studied the kindergarten curriculum files Tina had given her. Her teaching assistant had also been kind enough to note how far along in the program Ms. Cantor had gotten prior to leaving. The substitute had been operating out of a generic "sub plan" folder, which had kept the kids entertained and engaged, but hadn't specifically advanced the Standards of Learning put forth by the Virginia Department of Education.

She'd stayed up late last night thoughtfully fleshing out her strategy for the rest of this quarter, and then the year. Once she had the broad framework set, she could worry about her specific lessons by tackling those on a weekly basis. Mary Ellen was especially excited to be teaching at an international magnet school that focused on other cultures, and encompassed foreign language instruction for the children. She found the school's focus both globally relevant and forward thinking, and was happy to have joined the Turtle Creek team.

Like the other grade teachers at the school, she'd be afforded planning time during the day while her students were at their "specials": art, music, computing, PE, and foreign language, which included Chinese and Spanish. This would free up her evenings for grading assessments and homework. The academic part, she felt fully in control of. It was the personal side of things that had sent Mary Ellen's emotions out of kilter. It set her oddly on edge that she and Principal Johnson were seeing each other over the weekend. In the most innocent way, of course. Plus, Emma would be along, so it could hardly be considered a date.

Mary Ellen's fingers tightened around the steering wheel as she recalled learning that Wes was a widower. While part of her heart had ached for him and Emma and their tragic loss, another sneaky little side of her ticker had begun beating overtime. Even before she realized Wes was her boss, she'd felt so horrible about being attracted to a married man. But Wes wasn't married! He was single and attractive, and....*goodness gracious, Mary Ellen*—she mentally chided herself— also her direct supervisor.

She had to get a grip and put any notions of a relationship with Wes well out of her mind. Not that he'd be interested in becoming romantically involved with her anyway. The man still wore his wedding ring. That sent a message loud and clear: Wes wasn't ready to move on.

Which was perfect, actually. Because neither was Mary Ellen. She'd had a bad time in Surry and was still getting over it. She was also still recovering from spending *four long months* with her mother in DC. Thank heavens she'd come to her senses and had started applying to teaching jobs after the start of the year. Landing a job in October had been a long shot. Yet, Mary Ellen had lucked out and secured this marvelous position in Paradise, Virginia. All she had to do now was get on with her day...and try to avoid running into the principal.

She'd spent half the night dreaming about him, and the other half punching her pillow and fighting insomnia. It was hard to decide which was worse. Fantasizing about her boss kissing a dollop of ice cream off her lips, or being awake and realizing she'd *actually* dreamt that.

***

Wes started down the hall on his way to the cafeteria, then halted abruptly at the alarming ruckus. It was part cry and part shriek, rising shrilly on a chorus of "Eee-eye, eey-eye, ooooh..." That clearly wasn't his music teacher; it sounded almost like a sow giving birth. With all her little piglets chiming in! He caught Tina scurrying out of her classroom and stopped her with a query.

"Ms. Miller? What *is* that sound?"

She flushed brightly and stepped out of view of the doorway. "Our new teacher, sir. Miss Meeks!" She whispered hoarsely below the musical din. "*Leading her class in song.*"

"Ah." Wes angled forward and peered through the door at Miss Meeks's kindergarten class. She wasn't just singing, she was also leading the whole class around the room in an improvised conga line. All wore animal masks fashioned from paper plates, including Mary Ellen. She appeared to be a chicken. Wes stifled a chuckle. *Of course.* "Why aren't you in there joining in the fun?" he asked the teaching assistant.

"I thought now might be a good time for my break." Then she added hastily, "Miss Meeks said it was okay."

"Go right ahead." Wes stole another secretive peek at the happily parading class. "Miss Meeks certainly appears to have things under control." He couldn't help but note that Emma was a unicorn. Wes didn't recall that fictional beast being on Old McDonald's farm, though he decided it hardly mattered. Mary Ellen had apparently let the children choose what they wanted to be. He saw that Bobby was a giraffe, and Wilson a ferocious lion.

"She's priming the kids for their unit study of animals around the globe," Tina informed him. "She let each child pick their favorite animal at random, then the class will learn about that animal's natural habitat, and the country and culture it comes from. The idea was really quite clever. The kids are totally into it."

"Yes, yes. I see." Wes wondered how Mary Ellen was going to incorporate a unicorn into her curriculum, and was curious to find out.

"In any case…" Tina shrugged merrily. "I'm off for coffee now. Mary Ellen has us playing leap frog at recess, and I think I'll need my energy."

"No doubt," Wes said, grinning again. It was hard to believe it was Mary Ellen's first day. She was doing a spectacular job bonding with her class. What's more, she was already tapping into the curriculum. In an impressively unique and creative way. He still wondered about that unicorn, though…

He straightened his tie, focusing his gaze on the hallway before him. The double doors to the cafeteria were right ahead. Already, he could hear raucous hoots and hollers emerging. Wes hoped it wasn't those meddlesome fifth graders again, but he suspected it could be. That's why he needed to put in an appearance by making his rounds, before any trouble cranked up.

"Carry on, Ms. Miller," he said, tipping his chin her way. After she departed in the opposite direction, Wes threw back his head in a chortle. That Mary Ellen Meeks definitely was something. It appeared she was going to be a true asset here. She was innovative and fun, and… *prettier than anyone I've ever seen in a chicken mask.*

Wes paused with his hand halfway to the cafeteria swinging door. He definitely needed to stop thinking about Mary Ellen that way. She was his employee and a professional colleague, plain and simple.

Yeah, right. He swallowed past the lump in his throat. That would be totally easy to believe if he didn't privately feel like he'd already scheduled a date with her. But it wasn't a date! It was an appointment. *Sure.* They'd merely arranged to work on a mutual project together. Wes needed to keep looking it that way, without hunting for imagined trouble. His gaze snagged on his wedding band and it glinted in the fluorescent light. All at once he was sorry he'd passed Mary Ellen's classroom and caught a glimpse of her interacting with the children. If he thought he'd liked her before, her apparent ease as a teacher made him attracted to her even more.

Mary Ellen was more than competent. There was a sunny warmth about her that drew the students to her like moths to a flame. Wes worried that he was also getting sucked in. At a velocity he found troubling. Troubling and well, okay... He'd admit it. Perhaps just a tiny bit exciting, too. Mary Ellen was unusual and charming. Different from anyone he'd ever met. There was a goodness about her, besides. Something very earthy and real.

Maybe the best thing to do would be to keep his distance for a while. Just until he figured out how to better handle his current circumstances, including his upcoming appointment on Saturday. Building a chicken coop was one thing. Going for ice cream seemed a step beyond. Boy-oh-boy, wouldn't his sister Jenny have a field day with this. She hadn't seen him out with a single woman since Patricia passed.

Even if he explained his connection to Mary Ellen as a neighbor and mentioned her being Emma's teacher, Jenny was sure to say something. Wes just hoped she wouldn't say it in front of Mary Ellen. Because Wes was taking her to Cherry on Top. He'd as much as promised Emma, and an element of being a good dad was keeping your promises.

Chapter Six

MARY ELLEN THOUGHT it was strange that she'd
been teaching at Turtle Creek Elementary for four full
days now, and she'd barely laid eyes on the principal
while in the building. She'd passed by his office several
times, but each time that the door had been left open
the room had been empty. Since she'd begun teaching
on Tuesday, she'd only spotted Wes at work twice.
Once, on Wednesday afternoon as he'd hustled down
the hall toward the cafeteria during fifth-grade
lunchtime. He'd nearly bumped into her, as she exited
her classroom, taking her kids to art. He'd excused
himself with a flushed face, then he'd quickly hurried
on his way.

The second time was yesterday morning when
he'd brought a pair of parents by her classroom. They
were considering enrolling their child in the school, so
had come by to meet with the principal and receive a
tour. As their daughter was beginning kindergarten

next fall, Wes briefly showed them all three kindergarten classes. Mary Ellen wasn't sure if it was her imagination or not, but Wes's whole countenance seemed to redden as he introduced her, calling her "our wonderful new addition to the staff."

He'd had the same look when she'd seen him on the street each morning as he stood with Emma waiting for the school bus. Mary Ellen was typically pulling out of her driveway at that time, so would offer a wave and smile at them both. Emma always waved cheerily in return, but Wes just slowly lifted a hand, his grin pasted on tight.

Wes apparently drove himself in after putting Emma on the bus. As his direct commute was shorter than the school bus ride he arrived ahead of the children. Mary Ellen understood why Wes felt it was important for Emma to ride the bus with the other kids, so she could adjust to the routine and foster those important early grade school friendships, and Mary Ellen admired Wes's decision. He also let Emma ride the bus in the afternoon, and because of the similar transportation lag time, was able to get home first. Mary Ellen had missed seeing them this week during the afternoons, because her schedule had been so packed with errands. Even though her classroom was well-supplied with the basics, she had extra items she wanted to buy for school projects, and needed to pick up things for the house.

There was no shower curtain in the second bathroom for example, and the mini blinds in the living room were bent and needed replacing. Just as she suspected she would, she'd also run out of chicken feed. She'd make a return trip to the Horse and Hay Feed and Seed to buy more this afternoon on her way home.

Mary Ellen packed up her teaching bag and grabbed her purse out of her desk drawer, preparing to shut down her classroom for the weekend. It was Friday afternoon, and overall, she felt like she'd gotten off to a really fine start in her new position. By now, she comfortably knew all the children's names and had begun forming a pleasant working relationship with Tina, who was very friendly and helpful. Despite her diminutive size, Tina was also adept at controlling the kids. One sternly arched eyebrow could silence them within seconds.

Though most of the time Tina was smiling broadly. She appeared to love her job and had been at it for more than twenty years now. Her own kids were grown and in college, so she enjoyed being around the "little people" who kept her young. Tina's version of a

youth tonic certainly seemed to be working. Mary Ellen
had initially thought Tina was in her late thirties, but
was later surprised to hear she was nearly fifty. Tina
attributed her youthful appearance to the athletic tasks
involved in scrambling after kindergartners, which she
maintained kept her fit.

Mary Ellen turned off the light and locked her
classroom door. Tina generally left right after the kids
did. While Mary Ellen walked the bus riders and
students being picked up by car to the circular drive at
the front of the school, Tina took the contingent of kids
who were enrolled in the after-school program to the
cafeteria where it was hosted. Tina departed from
there, as she customarily parked at that end of the
building. Mary Ellen liked returning to her classroom
and having a bit of uninterrupted time to go over her
notes and briefly review her lessons for the next
teaching day, so she could have any needed
instructional items ready.

She passed the secretary in the front office on
her way out the door, and called merrily, "Have a good
weekend, Becky!"

Becky looked up from her computer work and
grinned. "Yeah, darling. You, too!"

Mary Ellen stepped into the sunshine, savoring its warmth on her face and in her hair. She wore a light jacket over nice slacks and a sweater today. The weather was getting cooler, and the air was nice and crisp, with big white clouds billowing in the bright blue sky. She could see farm fields in the distance and the tumbling hills of the surrounding mountains beyond those. Since it was a magnet school and students got in by application, rather than being assigned here due to residential zoning, Turtle Creek Elementary wasn't located in a particular school district. Instead, it was situated out in the country, about twenty minutes from the center of town. It was only a ten minute drive to Mary Ellen's house, though, since Sweetheart Valley Hills sat to the west of the urban area, just as this school did.

She inhaled deeply, taking in the scent of fresh-cut hay from a nearby farm, as fluttering foliage burned in vibrant autumn colors around her. Brittle leaves crowded low-hanging limbs forming a shady canopy over the parking area. Mary Ellen noted the spot reserved for the principal was vacant. She hoped Wes hadn't changed his mind about building that chicken coop tomorrow. Although she'd become more skilled at keeping Crazy contained, Mary Ellen still needed it badly. The rooster had nearly escaped *three* times by trying to fly over the fence. Fortunately, each time she'd caught him!

The poor animal likely had excess energy from being left caged in such a small space hour after hour. A large coop in the yard would certainly be better, as long as Mary Ellen could provide Crazy with a warm place to tuck into when the elements raged. She dropped her teaching bag in the trunk of her car then got into the driver's seat, pulling her cell from her purse, thinking that she should call Wes since they hadn't set a time for meeting tomorrow. That's when she recalled she didn't have Wes's cell number. *Well, gosh.* She'd have to drop by his house in that case. Mary Ellen clearly wanted to be presentable when Wes and Emma showed up for their Saturday project. Wes had already seen Mary Ellen in her giant pink curler once, and she was sure that was more than enough for any man.

***

Wes stacked his final piece of lumber on the dolly that already held a roll of chicken wire. He had plenty of nails and tools at home. "Are we going to build Crazy a house, Daddy?" Emma asked as they headed for the checkout. Wes smiled down at his daughter. Right after meeting her school bus, he'd brought her with him to the Horse and Hay Feed and Seed. The large warehouse building was stocked with all sorts of farming and gardening supplies, and smelled of potting soil, sawdust, and freshly sawed boards. "You bet we are," Wes answered. "Complete with a chicken roost!"

Emma's little face screwed up. "What's a chicken roost?"

"A shelf that Crazy can perch on. I'm going to build one in his house."

Emma seemed to be pondering something as she walked diligently beside him. After a moment, she glanced up, a question in her eyes. "Is that's why Crazy's called a rooster? Because he sits on a roost?"

Wes stared at his daughter in surprise. He'd never exactly thought about it, but it could be Emma had a point. "I'm not sure." He paused to consider this further. "We'll have to look it up."

The small child nodded eagerly. "We can do that when we're researching unicorns!"

Oh right, the project, Wes thought to himself, remembering Mary Ellen's lesson.

"That's my homework," Emma informed him happily. "I have to find out where unicorns come from!"

Wes kindly surveyed his daughter. "Well, that could be a task!"

"I have a homework sheet to fill in and everything," Emma added.

"I'll be sure to take a look when we get home."

Wes lined up at the register and Emma peered past him with a happy grin. "Look! It's Miss Meeks!"

Wes turned in surprise to see Mary Ellen ambling toward the register in labored strides. She clutched an enormous bag of chicken feed in her arms and its edges were poking out sideways, bumping into other customers as she passed them and banging into things hanging from hooks and on shelves. "Oops! Oh! Sorry!" she told an elderly gentleman who scowled her way, after she'd nearly knocked a ceramic planter from his grasp.

She bumped another guy on the backside then burned bright red when he spun on his heel. "Whoops! Apologies! Didn't mean it!"

Mary Ellen over-corrected, tilting the bag in the other direction, but the heavy weight of it slid in her grasp further. "Argh! Yikes!" She let out a yelp as two garden trowels and a small spade became dislodged from their hooks and crashed to the cement floor. She was going to lose the chicken feed next. And, if that fifty-pound bag split open...

Wes dashed to the rescue, nabbing the bulging bag just in time. "Here, let me!"

"Wes!" Mary Ellen met his gaze and the strap of her purse slipped from her shoulder, sliding all the way down into the crook of her elbow. Her purse dangled from it like a pendulum. Swinging back and forth, and back and forth...

Emma darted forward and stilled it before it knocked over a decorative garden gnome in a nearby display. "Emma, hi!" Mary Ellen blinked and stared down at her then back over at Wes, now holding her chicken feed. Emma slowly released her purse and beamed up happily. "Hi, Miss Meeks! Daddy and I were just talking about unicorns."

"Unicorns! Right!" Mary Ellen flushed brightly. "I'm so sorry about that... I really didn't know it was that heavy! Should have gotten a cart!" She heaved a breath, an apparent bundle of nerves. "What I mean is..." Mary Ellen exhaled sharply. "Thank you. Thank you both for your help!" She fumbled for her purse strap, repositioning it on her shoulder.

People were stepping around them and some were sharing pointed looks, owing to the fact that Wes was holding up the line. "Why don't you let me set this down on the counter?" Wes offered, seeing there was space for it.

"Hey!" a lady called from the aisle. She had a dolly of her own that was chock full of plumbing supplies. There were two customers waiting their turn between her and Wes. "That woman's butting in line!"

"No worries," Wes replied with a pleasant smile. "The chicken feed is mine."

"I can't let you..." Mary Ellen began in a whisper.

"We'll settle up later," Wes whispered back.

The irritated customer set a hand on her hip. "Maybe if you and your wife had picked things out *before* getting in line, you wouldn't have held things up."

Wife? Wes's ears burned hot, as Emma gave the complainer a toothless grin.

"They're not married!" she shouted back and the lady gasped.

"Well, then," the customer replied judgmentally. "Let's hope you're setting the right example for your little one." She said it addressing

Mary Ellen, as if she'd assumed Mary Ellen to be Emma's mother. Mary Ellen blinked in incredulity, apparently at a loss about what to say.

Wes quickly settled the bill, then uttered sotto voce, "Come on, let's get out of here."

As the threesome headed out the door, Wes called over his shoulder. He was pushing the dolly which now also held Mary Ellen's chicken feed. "Have a nice day!"

Before the sliding glass door shut behind him, he heard a distinct *harrumph*.

Mary Ellen arched her eyebrows, and his forehead rose in return.

"Why was that lady so grumpy, Daddy?" Emma wanted to know.

"Maybe she was having a bad day?" Mary Ellen offered.

Wes viewed her admiringly. "Hmm, yeah. Maybe so." He wheeled the dolly toward the parking lot, and turned to Mary Ellen.

"Which car is yours?"

"The white hatchback," she said, indicating the small sedan. "Over there."

Wes nodded and rolled the dolly toward it.

Mary Ellen opened her purse. "Now, how much do I owe you? For the feed and the chicken coop supplies?"

He considered her lovely face, feeling suddenly generous-spirited. "Why don't we just say this one's on me?"

Color swept her cheeks. "Oh, no. I couldn't let you do that. You're already helping with the construction."

"But *you're* buying the ice cream," he added with a twinkle. Wes suddenly realized he was looking forward to the outing in town. Whether or not it encouraged grief from his sister. Wes was tough enough to handle it.

"Of course! But that hardly seems enough..." A grin warmed her pretty face as she seemed to arrive at an idea. "How about dinner?"

"Dinner?" Wes asked, slightly thrown. While he'd envisioned spending part of Saturday with Mary Ellen, he hadn't imagined their time together stretching into the evening.

"Oh, boy! Daddy, can we?" Emma peered up at him with a hopeful gaze and Wes's heart hammered.

"I make a mighty mean spaghetti." Mary Ellen smiled and his heart hammered harder. "It's the least I can do." She withdrew her keys from her purse, and popped open her hatchback. "After all that you're doing for Crazy."

Wes hefted the feedbag into her car and eyed her cautiously. "Dinner sounds great. If you're sure?"

"Sure, I'm sure," Mary Ellen said brightly. "It will be a nice way to end the day."

A day that was sounding more and more date-like as time went on, Wes found himself thinking, his gaze skirting the wedding band on his hand. "All right, then," he agreed. "We have a..." Wes shut the hatchback with slightly too much force. "D...deal."

Mary Ellen boldly stuck out her hand. "A deal it is," she said, smiling.

Wes took her hand and a current ripped through him. A hot sexy buzz that raced right up his arm and sent fire to the pit of his belly. *Whoa.* That was heady stuff. Wes hadn't experienced that sort of chemical jolt since... Well, in forever. He hoped he was doing the right thing by spending more time with Mary Ellen, and not making his life more complicated. He had Emma to think of. He sent a cursory glance at his daughter, knowing he'd need to keep her well-being at the forefront of his mind. If Emma believed that he and Mary Ellen were simply friends and work associates that should be fine. There was no harm in making more friends in Sweetheart Valley Hills, and Wes could model being a good neighbor.

"We'll look forward to it," Wes told Mary Ellen. "Is starting around nine too early for you?"

Her blue eyes sparkled as she released his hand. "Nine a.m. sounds fine."

Chapter Seven

MARY ELLEN DASHED around her kitchen making sure she had things in good order. She'd prepared coffee but hadn't set it to brew. If Wes wanted a cup, she could have it ready in just a few minutes. She'd also baked homemade whole wheat apple walnut muffins, a loaf of pumpkin bread, and gluten-free oatmeal cookies, just in case Wes had this special dietary requirement. Since Emma was in her class, she knew the child didn't have any food allergies, but Mary Ellen wasn't so certain about Emma's dad. She paused and heaved a breath, tucking a strand of hair that had broken free from her ponytail behind one ear.

Her whole house smelled heavenly and very autumn-like. She hoped she'd made it seem homey, rather than like she'd been trying too hard. Which, in truth, she might have been. Mary Ellen had been inordinately nervous about this get-together ever since running into Wes and Emma at the Horse and Hay

Feed and Seed. When that stranger had intimated that Mary Ellen was Wes's wife, her internal temperature had soared. Then, there'd been that strange way Wes had looked at her in the parking lot, right when he'd taken her hand.

There'd been a spark of something in his eyes, something akin to manly interest. The sort a guy sometimes unintentionally displays when he's totally into a girl. Not that Wes was *totally* into Mary Ellen. Just as she clearly wasn't into him! That would be silly—stupid—for her to go crushing on her new boss simply because she'd learned he was single, hence eligible, and conveniently lived right across the street. It didn't hurt that Wes was also gorgeous, and kind, and obviously a very doting dad to precious Emma.

Crazy squawked in his cage, expanding his wings as he curiously peered out through the wire.

"You're getting a new home today," she told him. "Hopefully, one you'll like much better."

Crazy lowered his wings and dropped his head, and for a moment Mary Ellen almost thought he looked mournful. But that couldn't be right! Birds couldn't really display feelings, could they? And, surely, she was doing the right thing? A coop in the yard would give her pet plenty of room to roam. Plus, Wes had mentioned he'd be fashioning a birdhouse of some kind to provide shelter for Crazy when he needed it.

The doorbell rang, and Mary Ellen's heart raced. She checked the clock on the stove seeing it was exactly nine a.m. Wes and Emma were right on time.

***

But when Mary Ellen pulled back the door, she saw it wasn't the Johnsons at all. It was the disgruntled shopper from the Horse and Hay Feed and Seed!

"Uh, hello?" Mary Ellen queried uncertainly as the smile fell from her face. She'd answered the door all bright and bubbly, only to be torpedoed by this blast from her very recent past. If it was any consolation, the short, squat woman with wiry silver hair and ominous dark eyes appeared equally stunned to see Mary Ellen.

"My name is Calista Cartwright. And I'm your neighbor to the south. That means I live right behind you," she explained further. "Beyond your back fence."

"Er...great. That's nice!" Mary Ellen fumbled with her etiquette. "Would you like to come in?"

"Well, only for a minute. We have some business to address."

Mary Ellen couldn't believe Calista had hunted her down, all over Mary Ellen supposedly butting in line! "Mrs. Cartwright," she began gently, ushering the older woman inside. "If this is about the Horse and Hay—"

Calista's eyebrows arched sharply. "I thought you looked familiar, I just couldn't place where I'd seen you." She furtively glanced around the small living area that was decorated sparsely with low-end furnishings. A cheaply recovered sofa here...a plaid arm chair in the corner there, its cushion fraying at the front end... Simple lamps with dusty shades... Mary Ellen had meant to tend to those but she hadn't found the time. "He's not here, is he?"

"He?"

"Your gentleman friend," Calista said in a hushed whisper. Then she lowered her voice even further before adding, "You really should learn to be careful around your child."

"Mrs. Cartwright," Mary Ellen began. "I'm afraid you've gotten the completely wrong impression. Emma... I mean, the little girl...she's not mine. She's Wes Johnson's daughter."

Mrs. Cartwright met her gaze dead-on. "Wes Johnson?"

"He's the principal at Turtle Creek Elementary," Mary Ellen said, feeling the urge to defend him. "And a very fine gentleman, I assure you."

"A gentleman," Calista said skeptically. "I see."

Mary Ellen wasn't sure how to interpret this unusual neighborly visit, so she tried to make the most of it. "Can I offer you a cup of coffee?"

"No, thanks." Calista shook her head, apparently puzzling over something. "Mr. Johnson is single, I suppose?"

"Yes," Mary Ellen offered. "He's a widower, in fact."

"Poor dear." This seemed to soften Calista a tad. "How long has his wife been gone?"

"I'm...not exactly sure."

"And you two know each other how?"

Mary Ellen blinked at the brazen inquisition. Despite her better judgment, she felt compelled to answer. If Calista was implying there was something untoward about her relationship with Wes, Mary Ellen was prepared to set her nosy neighbor straight. Then again, she decided she shouldn't inform Calista that Wes lived right across the street. Calista might take it upon herself to go calling on him, too! "Wes and I work together," Mary Ellen said, offering up another truth.

Calista scrutinized her a beat. "How convenient for you both."

"Honestly, it's not like—"

"Whatever." Calista testily shook her head. "Mores have gone out the window these days, anyhow."

Mary Ellen was about to issue her rejoinder, but Calista barreled ahead. "And anyway, that's not what I came to talk about."

"It's not?" Mary Ellen asked, completely at a loss.

"Actually, it concerns your rental in Sweetheart Valley Hills." Calista narrowed her eyes and Mary Ellen's heart thumped. "I'm the president of our neighborhood association here, and I've received a complaint."

"A complaint?" Mary Ellen had been here less than two weeks. What on earth could she have done?

"Someone reported a crowing sound coming from your backyard."

"Crowing?" Mary Ellen asked weakly. To her knowledge, Crazy had only crowed once while outdoors, and that had been on Monday morning when she'd first met Wes. Crazy had startled at the sound of the departing school bus and let out a cry. Though the bus's rumble had been so loud, it was hard to believe anyone could have heard Crazy crow above it.

"Surely, you're not keeping livestock here. This is a city neighborhood."

"Well, I..."

"Because if you were," Calista continued ominously, "that could mean eviction, you know."

Eviction? Seriously? Mary Ellen held her breath and willed Crazy to stay very, very quiet. He'd been as good as gold so far. "I'll be sure to keep that in mind."

"So, you're not harboring a barn animal?" Calista challenged.

"Harboring? Well, er...no. He's not exactly a fugitive!"

"Aha! So you *do* have a bird!"

"No!" Mary Ellen panicked at the lie, but what else could she say? She couldn't get evicted. Nor could she get rid of Crazy! He was just started to get trained. Plus, she'd grown attached to him. He really was kind of cute in his own mischievous way.

"No?"

"Yes! I mean, you're right! The answer is, no!"

Calista narrowed her eyes into slits. "Mind if I have look around?"

Mary Ellen couldn't believe Calista's gall. She actually wanted to snoop in Mary Ellen's house? "I'm afraid things aren't very presentable." Without thinking, she stepped in front of the doorway to the kitchen, blocking Calista's view of it. "I haven't finished unpacking and the kitchen is a mess. Really dirty!"

"Oh?" Calista appeared horrified.

"I've been super busy. Haven't done the dishes in days."

"Ew!"

"I, er...unless that's another violation?"

"Is Mr. Johnson aware of your sanitary habits?" Calista appeared extremely faint. "Or, lack thereof?"

Just the mention of his name made Mary Ellen more anxious. He'd be arriving at any moment with Emma, and a big arm-load of chicken wire! "You said the complaint was about my backyard?" Mary Ellen asked, thinking quickly.

"Your backyard, yes. The complaining party was quite sure the noise had come from there."

"Well, I can show it to you, if you'd like? Would that help?"

Calista eyed her skeptically. "Well, yes. I suppose it would." She attempted to peer past Mary

Ellen. "Is the door to the outside through there?" she asked, pointing to the kitchen's glass door to the patio.

"Oh, no! Let's not go that way!"

When Calista viewed her quizzically, she added, "Who knows what sort of bacteria is lurking in the air."

Calista paled. She brought her fist to her mouth, appearing mildly sick to her stomach. "Yes, yes, of course. Wouldn't want to risk it."

"We'll go around front!" Mary Ellen cracked open the front door and poked her head outside, scanning Wes's house across the street. He and Emma were just emerging from his garage, loaded down with gear. Wes held a huge roll of chicken wire and several boards, while Emma pulled a wagon filled with supplies. Mary Ellen would need to make haste in getting Calista out of here.

Fortunately there was a gate at the rear of her property, so perhaps she could get Calista to depart that way to keep her from running into Wes. "We'd best get going, Mrs. Cartwright!" she said brightly and the older woman blinked. "I'm afraid I've got an appointment in a bit."

Her neighbor followed her blankly out the door as Mary Ellen kept trying to hurry her along. "You should have mentioned your appointment earlier," Calista said. "When I first showed up."

Mary Ellen smiled deferentially and opened the side gate. "I didn't want to be rude."

They reached the back lawn and Mary Ellen gave a broad sweep of her arm. "You see? Nothing here! No chickens!"

Calista's eagle-like gaze skirted around the yard, landing on the patio and carefully examining the perimeter of the fence. Mary Ellen was grateful she'd placed Crazy's cage against the wall to the left of the glass door; it remained concealed from this vantage point.

Calista's face sagged in disappointment as she curtly addressed Mary Ellen. "I suppose it's my turn to apologize. It appears the individual who filed the complaint was wrong."

Through the closed glass door to the kitchen, Mary Ellen could hear her front doorbell ringing inside the house. "Oh! I…"

"That must be your appointment," Calista said, appearing defeated. "Don't worry, I can let myself out." She eyed the back gate. "I'm sure Sheila won't mind if I cut through her yard."

"Sheila?" Mary Ellen asked, surprised. "But I thought you lived—"

"My house is directly opposite that one on Maple."

"I...I see."

"Sheila Wilcox and her husband Bob live right there behind you. But they never complain about a thing. Bob keeps their television going so loud, they almost never hear the doorbell." Mary Ellen wondered if that was true, or whether Sheila simply didn't want to answer the door when Calista was outside. "Or the phone ring, for that matter! Both have mostly lost their hearing," Calista further confided. "So I'm starting to doubt that either can hear much at all."

The doorbell rang again inside her house and Mary Ellen's pulse pounded. "Well, I guess I'd better run!" Yet, she was reluctant to leave Calista alone until she was securely through that gate.

"Sure. All right." To Mary Ellen's enormous relief, Calista finally strode toward the back gate. "Sorry to have troubled you," she offered, not sounding exactly convincing.

"No trouble! It was...ah...er...really great to meet you, Calista! I mean, officially." Her natural instinct was to say, *drop by at any time.* Instead, Mary Ellen firmly bit her tongue.

Then, the second the back gate latched, she slid back the glass door by the patio and raced inside.

***

Mary Ellen answered the door feeling frazzled. "Wes! I mean, Mr. Johnson and Em—"

"Wes is just fine here," he interrupted with a smile.

"Hi, Miss Meeks!" Emma chirped from a few feet behind him. She stood at the bottom of the stoop holding the handle to her loaded-down red wagon. It contained a toolbox, paintbrushes, and a few small cans of paint. Mary Ellen was surprised by this last part. Wes caught her eyes on the painting supplies and explained, "We thought you might like us to make a sign for Crazy's place of residence?" His green eyes sparkled. "It was Emma's idea."

"And what a wonderful idea it is!" Mary Ellen appreciatively told the child.

Wes indicated the spool of chicken wire and the boards he held in his arms. "Shall I carry these around back?"

"Around back would be great," Mary Ellen said, still catching her breath. She hoped her nosy neighbor wouldn't decide to make a return trip. What a close call that had been!

Wes nodded and herded Emma along. The child turned her wagon around with remarkable agility and followed him.

"See you on the other side!" Mary Ellen said, darting back inside the door. She strode quickly through her living room and into the kitchen, exiting by the sliding glass door. Wes stood beside Emma, who was latching the gate.

Wes glanced around the fenced backyard. "Where were you thinking?"

A row of stout shrubs flanked the right side of the patio when facing the yard from the kitchen. The separate fenced-in area housing the garbage can stood on the street side of that, adjoining the house. It had a side door leading into the garage and formed a buffer between the backyard and the front lawn. If Wes were to construct Crazy's coop between the trash area and the bushes by the patio, it wouldn't be visible from the street. It would be equally tough to spot from the abutting backyard, unless someone was specifically looking for it.

"How about over there?" she asked, pointing to the section she'd selected. Mary Ellen wasn't exactly out to dupe her neighbors, but she certainly didn't want anyone carting Crazy away. She'd been working hard to tame him and had already taught him to sit complacently on her lap while she petted him. Though it was true that he could only hold that pose for roughly five minutes, Mary Ellen nonetheless believed she'd been making progress in getting her pet to trust her. A rooster wasn't quite as cuddly as a kitten, but Crazy did appear to appreciate Mary Ellen's company in his own peculiar way.

"Looks like a good spot," Wes agreed. "Should get the morning sun and the afternoon shade."

As he hauled his gear in that direction, Mary Ellen asked whether he'd like coffee, offering to also supply a cold drink for Emma. "How about if we take a break in a bit?" Wes beamed at her graciously and Mary Ellen's heart fluttered. If she thought he looked handsome in his jacket and tie, he somehow seemed even sexier wearing his plaid flannel shirt and jeans.

Emma wore jeans and a sweatshirt, while Mary Ellen had donned jeans and a sweater. It was a gorgeous fall morning: sunny and warm, with a light breeze sifting through the stand of pines her neighbors had planted on the other side of the fence. The trees afforded additional privacy for the chicken coop location that was appearing more and more ideal.

Wes set down his load and beckoned Emma over with her wagon. Then he squatted low, preparing to work. He rolled up one shirt sleeve and then the other, exposing his toned and tanned forearms. For a guy who worked at a desk job, Wes was incredibly fit, with a solid build that was lean yet muscled.

"Let's map out exactly where you want this," he said. "Then we can get to work." He turned to his daughter. "Tape measure?"

Emma nodded obediently and opened the black toolbox in the bright red wagon. She located the tape measure in the tray on top and carried it to him. Next, he addressed Mary Ellen with earnest green eyes. "Ready to make a palace for Crazy?"

Mary Ellen laughed. "A palace might be a bit of a stretch. But I suppose just as long as he's the king of his castle..." Her lips twisted wryly and Wes chuckled in response.

"I think we can work with that." He cast a sideways glance at his daughter. "Can't we, Emma?"

The child's face lit up in a grin. "Uh-huh!"

"I'm happy to help," Mary Ellen added, dangling the hammer from its handle in a joke.

"Super!" Wes said. "Grab some nails. The long ones in the third compartment over will do."

***

A few hours later, Wes proudly observed their creation. They'd constructed a small house with a slanted roof and a shelf inside that could serve as a roost. He and Emma had learned that roosters were so called due to their habit of *roosting*, or sitting on a high perch so they could oversee and defend their designated group of nesting hens. As they worked, they shared this information with Mary Ellen, and she claimed to find it incredibly interesting.

Wes installed a hanging rubber flap to serve as the door to the chicken house, explaining that it could easily be pushed aside by the brawny bird when he was entering or leaving his special enclave. At other times, it could help buffer the wind. Wes had dashed back across the street for the extra hay he had in his garage from his fall lawn-seeding project, and asked Emma to line the floor of Crazy's house and his roost with it.

"It looks amazing!" Mary Ellen said, admiring the structure. Wes couldn't help but think that she looked pretty amazing herself. Her long blond hair was up in a ponytail today, and her chocolate-colored crew-neck sweater showed a hint of a white blouse collar underneath. Her simple attire, which included jeans and sneakers, outlined her trim—yet womanly—figure. Wes hadn't considered the curves of a woman's body in a long time. Not in the way he was thinking of now, which involved holding that beautiful body up against his as he took Mary Ellen in his arms. Wes yanked a hanky from his hip pocket to dab the back of his neck, which was suddenly scorching hot.

"We're not done yet," he told her, shoving his hanky back in his pocket. "We've got the wire fencing to put in."

"And the sign!" Emma added helpfully.

"Yes, there's that." Wes lovingly considered his daughter, who'd been such a big help handing him nails and such, while Mary Ellen had assisted by holding the boards steady. "How are you doing, hon? Are you ready for a break?"

Emma rubbed her belly. "I am a little hungry."

Mary Ellen smiled brightly at Emma and then at Wes. "I've got the perfect snack indoors."

Chapter Eight

EMMA SELECTED AN apple walnut muffin and Wes opted for a slice of pumpkin bread to go with his coffee. "These baked goods look delicious," he told Mary Ellen, as he and Emma sat at her kitchen table. She poured Emma a cold glass of milk at the counter as Crazy watched them with interest from the confines of his cage.

"I hope you enjoy them." She brought the glass of milk over and set it down by Emma, who thanked her. "I was in a bit of a baking mood this morning."

Wes glanced around the kitchen, taking in the aromatic scents that still lingered in the air. "I can see that." Mary Ellen's kitchen smelled warm and inviting. Homey. Even with a chicken sitting in the corner. "Thanks for making us two of your benefactors."

She served the coffee and joined them at the table. "Thanks for building Crazy's coop!"

"You're welcome."

Wes took a bite of pumpkin bread and the tasty morsel nearly melted in his mouth. "This pumpkin bread is out of this world," he said, meaning it absolutely. While he routinely made home-cooked meals for Emma, Wes very rarely baked. So this was a definite treat.

"You're getting a new home soon," Emma told Crazy with a giggle.

He fluttered out his wings and Emma giggled again. "I think Crazy's happy."

Though it was a bit nutty to think it, Wes wondered if Emma was right. The rooster was very bright-eyed and somehow seemed extra alert. He evidently was observing the humans carefully and enjoying their interactions. "He'll be even happier once he starts getting more sunshine," Wes said. Then he hastily added, "Not that you haven't been doing a fine job looking after him, Mary Ellen."

"It's all right," she said kindly. "I know exactly what you mean. He's a country animal, and country animals naturally need fresh air."

"I like the country!" Emma crowed. "There are cows there!"

"Yes, that's true," Mary Ellen agreed.

"My parents own a big farm on the outskirts of Paradise," Wes explained. "Emma and I used to spend a lot of time there."

Mary Ellen's eyebrows rose as she sipped from her coffee. "Do your parents still live at the farm?" She'd chosen an oatmeal cookie for herself and now took a dainty nibble.

"Actually, no. They still keep their old farmhouse as a rental, but they sold the dairy part of their business to the farm next door, the Smith Dairy. Ian Smith, who's married to my sister Jenny, took over running it for his parents a few years ago. Shortly afterwards, Jenny opened her ice cream shop."

"Cherry on Top!" Emma piped in.

Wes chuckled fondly at his daughter. "That's right. It's done really well and has become very popular with the locals."

"I can't wait to see it!"

"The ice cream's mighty tasty too," Wes informed her with a smile. "Isn't it, nugget?" He glanced at his daughter for confirmation, and Emma nodded enthusiastically.

"Where do your parents live now?"

"Since they've retired from farming, they wanted to live closer in. They bought a bungalow downtown in a neighborhood where they can walk to all the shops."

"That sounds nice."

Wes knew it did, but he still couldn't help the mild melancholy that came over him at the thought of losing Misty Meadows. He'd grown up on that farm and he'd loved it. In some ways Wes had always imagined he'd provide that sort of life for his own family one day, but when he'd married Patricia she'd been much more of a city girl. The suburbs were about as far out in the country as she'd been willing to move.

"The house Jenny and I grew up in sits on about ten acres now," Wes continued. "I guess you could call it a mini farm. You couldn't plant much in that space, but you could keep a horse there. The current renters have two."

"Your folks are keeping the property as an investment, then?"

Wes gave a half-hearted smile. "In truth, I'm not sure they can bear to sell it. Each time the topic comes up, one of them or the other changes his or her mind. The land has been in the Johnson family for a number of years, and the original section of the farmhouse was built by my great-grandpa in the early nineteen hundreds."

Mary Ellen's eyes sparkled and Wes could tell she was trying to imagine it. "Sounds like a really cool place."

"It is."

"Have *you* ever considered—?"

"Years ago, I thought about it, sure. But you know..." Wes shrugged noncommittally. "Time passes."

"Sure does!" Mary Ellen said sunnily. She stood and offered to refill Wes's coffee cup.

"Don't think I'd better," he said. "I had a few cups of coffee at home this morning. You don't want me being too jazzed when I'm working with tools. Even hand tools."

Mary Ellen laughed lightly. "All right, and thank you. Thank you both again for all your help."

"It shouldn't take too much longer." Wes checked his watch. "Maybe about an hour to drive in the posts and put up the chicken wire. While I'm busy with that, Emma can make her sign."

The child shot Mary Ellen a toothless grin. "Will you help me, Miss Meeks?"

Mary Ellen refilled her coffee mug and sat back at the table. "You know what?" she said sweetly to Emma. "I'd love to!"

***

By twelve-thirty the entire project was done. Mary Ellen marveled at how expertly Wes had put everything together, with little Emma acting as his eager apprentice. Mary Ellen had helped too, of course, but Emma was a natural-born handywoman. Wes had an easy way with his daughter that Mary Ellen appreciated. He was firm in issuing his requests and giving directions, but at the same time loving and kind. Mary Ellen guessed that being a single dad on top of having a demanding job as a principal was challenging for Wes. Yet he appeared to be maintaining a balance between work and family with incredible finesse.

Wes eyed the wide board onto which Emma had painted Crazy's name in big red letters, with gentle guidance from Mary Ellen of course. "Your sign looks marvelous, Emma!"

The girl beamed happily. "Miss Meeks helped."

"Oh, but just a tiny bit," Mary Ellen protested kindly.

"We should let the sign dry completely before I install it," Wes said. Prior to Emma and Mary Ellen's paint job, he'd hammered the signboard to a wooden stake he intended to drive into the ground by the front entrance to Crazy's coop, which was actually a small swinging door in the chicken wire.

"How about if we set the sign out in the sun while we have lunch?" Mary Ellen inquired.

A pleased grin crossed Wes's face. "Lunch?"

"We certainly can't have ice cream without eating something healthy first." Mary Ellen spoke in official sounding tones and Emma giggled.

"Yeah, Daddy. Lunch before dessert!"

Wes viewed Mary Ellen uncertainly. "But we're already putting you out for dinner. Two meals in one day—"

"Plus a snack!" Emma put in and Wes's neck colored.

"Yes, plus that."

"Don't be silly," Mary Ellen countered. "I made the spaghetti sauce up last night, so that's ready to go. And, it will only take a couple of minutes to put a few simple sandwiches together. What do you fancy?" she asked Emma with a sparkle. "Peanut butter and jelly or grilled ham and cheese?"

***

After a simple lunch, Wes helped Mary Ellen load the dirty dishes in her dishwasher, contemplating how domestic this occasion seemed. Since Wes hadn't really dated since losing Patricia, playing house with another woman made him slightly uneasy, even though he knew rationally that it shouldn't. He and Mary Ellen weren't seeing each other romantically. They were merely neighbors and colleagues who were forming a friendship. Mary Ellen was awfully good with Emma, too. Probably in part due to her practice in dealing with kids as a teacher.

"Thanks for the lunch," he told her. "I don't know when I last had grilled ham and cheese. It was delicious."

"Yeah," Emma happily agreed. "My peanut butter and jelly, too!"

"I'm glad you both could join me." Mary Ellen smiled pleasantly then glanced down at Crazy's cage. "What do you think? Should we introduce Crazy to his new coop?"

"Now sounds like a great time," Wes remarked. "I can put the sign up once we get back from having our ice cream."

When Mary Ellen took the rooster from his cage, Emma asked shyly, "Can I pet him?"

"Sure," Mary Ellen said, bringing him closer to the girl. She cradled the big bird in her arms and bent forward toward Emma. The child gently stroked the back of Crazy's neck and he let out a soft coo. Mary Ellen smiled at the child. "I think Crazy likes you, Emma."

A hopeful expression graced Emma's face. "Can I play with him outside?"

Mary Ellen cast a sidelong look at Wes. "If your father thinks it's all right."

Wes nodded and Emma's eyes lit up. "Oh, boy!"

"I'm sure he'd like to run around a bit before getting placed in the coop," Mary Ellen said. "He has been penned up all morning."

She set Crazy down on the floor and Emma beckoned. "Come on, Crazy!" The rooster toddled after her as she walked toward the sliding glass door.

"We'd probably better stick close," Mary Ellen whispered to Wes. "In case Crazy decides to make another break for it."

He chuckled in response, reflecting on what a good time he was having. "Yeah."

Mary Ellen slid back the door and Emma darted out onto the patio. Crazy picked up his pace trotting after her. "Let's pretend I'm your mommy!" Emma said to the bird. "You follow me!"

But instead of obeying, the rooster apparently had another idea. He took off running in the opposite direction, hustling around the corner of the house. Both Mary Ellen and Wes lit out after him, but little Emma was in hot pursuit first.

"Crazy, come back here!" Mary Ellen called.

"He thinks it's some kind of game," Wes observed.

"Yeah!" Emma chirped. "He wants to play tag!"

The group rounded the corner to find Crazy standing by the door to his new coop. "Well, well, well..." Wes gave a hearty chuckle. "It looks like this rooster found his way home."

Mary Ellen indicated the sign that had been drying in the sun. "Leaving a few impressions along the way." Wes goggled at the sign, seeing the letters of Crazy's name were marred by tiny rooster claw prints.

"Don't worry," he told the others. "We can fix it."

"Maybe we shouldn't?" Mary Ellen shot him an impish smile, and his heart hammered. "I kind of like it that Crazy's put his own personal stamp on things." She turned toward the little girl. "What do you think, Emma?"

Emma grinned sunnily. "I *like* it!"

Chapter Nine

LATER THAT AFTERNOON, Wes, Emma, and Mary Ellen carried their ice cream cones to the town square. They'd stopped by Cherry on Top to say hi to Wes's sister and purchase their ice cream, which was Mary Ellen's treat at her insistence. Jenny Smith was a friendly woman about Mary Elle's age. She wore a brown ponytail and had stunning green eyes like her brother.

She'd smiled happily when she'd seen Wes and Emma enter her shop, and had seemed particularly pleased to meet Mary Ellen, whom Wes had introduced as his new neighbor and Emma's teacher. Though there hadn't been time for extended conversation due to the press of other customers waiting in line, Mary Ellen had enjoyed meeting Jenny. She'd also detected a warm bond between the siblings, and got the sense that Jenny was fond of teasing her older brother.

"How about we sit over there?" Wes asked, motioning toward a bench by the gurgling central fountain.

Emma sat happily, taking a big lick of her cone. She'd chosen Pumpkin Spice, while Wes had gotten Cinnamon Vanilla Custard, and Mary Ellen had selected the heavenly Gooey Chocolate Pecan Fudge.

Wes sat beside his daughter and Mary Ellen joined them, sitting on Emma's other side. "This ice cream is delicious," she said, savoring the chewy nougat and crunchy pecans as the silky smooth chocolate melted in her mouth. "I think this is the best I've ever...!"

Her voice fell off when she caught Wes staring at her in an odd way.

"What?" Mary Ellen asked, perplexed. "What is it?"

"You have the tiniest bit of chocolate right..." Wes slowly raised his napkin and Emma cupped her mouth with a giggle. "Here," Wes said, dabbing gently at a spot at the side of Mary Ellen's mouth. Heat seeped through her as she recalled her silly fantasy. The one that involved Wes kissing a smudge of ice cream off her lips...

"Oh, ah...sorry," she said as her cheeks continued to flame.

"No worries." Wes winked and her face burned hotter. "Happens to the best of us."

"Yes. Yes, I'm sure."

Wes must have gathered that he'd embarrassed her, because he kindly changed the subject. "Tell us about your last place. The place where you lived?"

"You mean, when I lived with my mother?" She certainly wasn't going to share about her dramatic poetry writing phase. Nor did she want to get into explaining about her mom not really being sick. That topic of discussion might only confuse and worry Emma. Mary Ellen would do better addressing that subject one-on-one with Wes later.

"I meant before that," Wes said, resting an elbow against the back of the bench. He'd nearly finished his ice cream and was already crunching into the cone.

Mary Ellen gave an inner sigh, grateful to be on more comfortable territory. "Oh, there! You mean, where I taught in Surry?"

"Yes," Wes answered. "Did you like it?"

"Oh yes," Mary Ellen said, smiling at the memories. "My school was really great. The kids were amazing and the administration was...tops." She swallowed hard, thinking her present administration was staring her straight in the eyes. And Wes's eyes were incredible, too.

He observed her briefly before saying, "Having a supportive administrator is a plus. I had one when I started teaching. Mr. Westin is the one who encouraged me to become a principal myself."

"Were you teaching at Turtle Creek?" she asked him.

Wes nodded cordially. "Fourth grade math and science."

"Do you miss being in the classroom at all?"

"Sometimes," he seemed to admit truthfully, "but for the most part I really love my job. Turtle Creek hasn't always been an international magnet school. Soon after I became the principal, I helped with the transition."

"How exciting!"

"It was..." He polished off his cone then self-corrected. "Is. Is still very exciting. I enjoy going in every day."

"They say that's the best type of job you can have," Mary Ellen commented.

"Do you feel the same way?" His gaze lingered on her a moment and Mary Ellen's breath quickened.

"About?"

The left half of his mouth tipped up in a grin. "Your job."

Mary Ellen immediately felt the fool. "My job! Of course! Yes, yes, I do. I love teaching kindergarten very much."

"And we love you," Emma said sweetly.

Mary Ellen blushed at the compliment and Emma's childhood innocence. "I love you, too," Mary Ellen told Emma. "And I absolutely adore being your teacher. I feel so lucky that you're in my class!"

"I hear we have an assignment this weekend," Wes added with a hearty chuckle. "Unicorn research."

"That's true," Mary Ellen agreed before adding mock-sternly to the child, "And I'll expect the full report..."

Little Emma rolled her eyes then recited as if by rote, "Where unicorns live, what unicorns eat, and where unicorns sleep..."

"Exactly!" Mary Ellen said, grinning brightly. Next, she addressed Wes in case he'd not yet had time to read the assignment paper. "I let all the kids pick their favorite animal for this project. The idea is for them to research with a parent then create a comic-strip-type drawing containing three individual panes. The first will show the animal's country of origin, the second will portray its diet, and the last will depict where it goes to sleep or rest."

Wes viewed her admiringly. "It's a wonderful assignment." His eyes twinkled tellingly. "I'm just not sure about finding information on unicorns."

"Use your imagination," Mary Ellen prodded lightly. "If you get stuck, I'm sure Emma will help you."

"Yeah, Daddy!" Emma slurped at her ice cream, some of which was melting and dripping down her hand. Mary Ellen grabbed her napkin to wipe it. At the same time, Wes leaned forward with his. All at once they were face to face, their noses nearly colliding into each other.

"Oh!" Mary Ellen jerked back, while Wes hurriedly dabbed Emma's hand.

"Excuse...me," he stammered, as his temples turned crimson.

Emma gawked at her dad, then arched her eyebrows at Mary Ellen. "Were you going to kiss my daddy?"

The blood drained from Mary Ellen's face and her head felt light. "No, sweetie. It was just an—"

"Accident!" Wes filled in. "Miss Meeks and I nearly bumped noses! Ha-ha! How silly was that?"

His child viewed him quizzically, then burst into giggles. "Pretty silly, yeah."

Wes glanced at Mary Ellen then quickly looked away. "Why don't you finish up your ice cream?" he suggested to Emma. "Then we can take a walk around. I'll bet Miss Meeks would really like to see the town, and now's a good time while it's still daylight."

Emma shrugged happily. "All right."

Wes slowly raised his eyes to Mary Ellen to find her staring at him. "Okay by you?"

Anything to put the embarrassing experience of nearly knocking noses behind her! "Absolutely," she said, finishing her cone.

***

The rest of the afternoon and evening passed pleasantly, with the trio enjoying each other's company. After giving Mary Ellen a walking tour of the quaint downtown area, Wes drove them back to Sweetheart Valley Hills, where Mary Ellen had a spaghetti dinner waiting at her place. She'd prepared things in advance, so was able to put the meal together quickly. Still,

Emma was yawning by the time the meal was served. It had been an eventful day, so Mary Ellen understood why the little girl was exhausted. Mary Ellen was a tad worn out herself. Though some of that had to do with the roller coaster of emotions she'd experienced ever since Wes had wiped that bit of ice cream off her chin.

He was so unbelievably handsome, and honorable, and giving and kind. It was hard not to be attracted to him as more than an administrator and a neighbor. Mary Ellen was developing feelings for him as a man. A very sexy and eligible man, who was currently pouring her a glass of wine. He'd grabbed a bottle from his kitchen after driving them back from downtown, and before they'd returned to her place for dinner. She'd been pleased by his thoughtful gesture, and had decided that having just one glass of Chianti wouldn't hurt the situation. Besides, it paired mighty well with her homemade garden spaghetti over angel hair pasta. She'd also made a simple side salad and toasted a baguette.

"Thank you for a wonderful day," Mary Ellen said, as Wes filled his own wineglass then set the bottle on the table between them. She'd lit the candle she always kept on the kitchen table and its cozy glow filled the room. It seemed a little lonely in here without

Crazy. She hoped he was adjusting okay to his new spot in the yard, but she could check on him after diner. "Thanks especially for your help building Crazy's coop." She smiled warmly at Wes then at Emma. "I'm sure he'll be much happier living out there during the day."

"He'll get used to spending nights outdoors, too," Wes assured her warmly. "That's what roosters were born to do."

"I liked getting ice cream!" Emma reported happily, digging into her pasta. "That was fun!"

"It was fun, wasn't it?" Wes glanced at Mary Ellen and his eyes sparkled. "Thank you for treating us."

"Anytime!" Mary Ellen took a slow sip of wine, thinking that not long ago she couldn't have imagined this. As a newcomer to Paradise she'd been so lonely at first. And look at her now, with these great new friends. Though, in her heart of hearts, Mary Ellen didn't feel like she was dining with mere casual acquaintances. In just one day, everything seemed to have changed.

Wes viewed her thoughtfully before starting his spaghetti. "You know, I've had a great time today, too. I mean that honestly. Better than..." He perplexedly shook his head. "Well, better than I can remember in a while."

Emma yawned and covered her mouth and Mary Ellen smiled softly. "Me too, but it seems it's been a long day for some of us."

Wes chuckled heartily. "It's probably been a long day for *all* of us." He stared at Mary Ellen and his gaze lingered, causing her heart to skip a beat.

She smiled thoughtfully. "I'm sure we'll all sleep well tonight."

"Hopefully, even Crazy." Wes dug into his food, swirling a big heap of sauce-covered pasta around his fork and lifting it to his mouth. "Mmm, phenomenal!" he said appreciatively. "Really great sauce."

Mary Ellen grinned, pleased. "I'm so happy you like it." After a beat she asked him, "Wes, do you know a neighbor named Calista Cartwright?"

His brow creased as he pondered her question. "Calista? Hmm... No, I can't say I do."

"She's the one who was at the Horse and Hay Feed and Seed."

"Her?" Wes stifled a laugh, nearly choking on his wine. "And she lives in Sweetheart Valley Hills?"

"Apparently, yes," Mary Ellen stated tentatively. "She stopped by early this morning to say..." Mary Ellen hesitated, thinking maybe she shouldn't bring this up around Emma.

"To say what?"

"Er...nothing," Mary Ellen offered, deciding to mention it to Wes in private later. "Just to welcome me to the neighborhood, that's all."

Wes eyed Mary Ellen astutely, and she shared a telling look.

"You'll have to tell me about it later," he said.

"Yes!"

Emma curiously viewed the adults. "It's not nice to keep secrets, Daddy says."

"It's not exactly a secret," Mary Ellen rushed in. "It's more like...something that you'd find incredibly boring." She pulled a face. "Grown-up talk and all that."

"Ohhh..." Emma gave a knowledgeable nod. "Like school board meetings."

Mary Ellen burst out in giggles. "Yeah! I suppose something like that." She glanced at Wes, who shared a sheepish grin.

"I'm afraid Emma's had to sit through a few of those. You know, on the nights when I couldn't get a sitter."

"Are sitters really that hard to find?" Mary Ellen inquired politely. "I'd think in a family neighborhood like this—"

"Let's just say I'm very picky," Wes said smoothly, and Mary Ellen couldn't blame Wes for being overprotective of his only daughter.

"Aunt Jenny babysits sometimes!" Emma piped in. "So do Grammy and Poppy."

"That's true." Wes took another heaping forkful of spaghetti. "It's nice having family nearby."

"Your sister seems very nice," Mary Ellen said, enjoying her dinner. She was pleased that it had come out so well.

"Thanks."

"Have you always been close?"

"Pretty much, yeah. Although..."

"What?"

Wes seemed to change his mind. "She just gets into my business sometimes, that's all. But, that's what siblings do." He tilted his head her way. "How about you? Any brothers or sisters?"

"It's just me and my mom."

"I'm so glad she's doing better."

Emma frowned worriedly then asked Mary Ellen, "Is your mommy sick?"

"No, honey! She's just fine! As fit as a fiddle!"

Wes whispered across the table when Emma's head was turned, "Sorry."

"It's okay," Mary Ellen whispered back. She was definitely going to need to straighten Wes out about the mom thing, and soon. Though it wouldn't be tonight, because their youngest group member was fading fast. Emma's eyelids drooped and she slumped forward over her plate. Wes reached out his hand and steadied her little shoulder.

"You two should probably run along," Mary Ellen said softly.

Emma opened her eyes and blinked. "I'm sleepy."

Wes spoke warmly and pushed back his chair. "I know, honey. It's getting past bedtime for you." He stared around the table at the nearly empty plates. They'd almost finished anyway, but he hated leaving Mary Ellen with the mess.

"I'll handle the cleanup here," Mary Ellen offered kindly.

"I owe you," Wes said with a wink, and Mary Ellen's skin tingled all over.

Wes got to his feet and picked up his child. She wrapped her arms around his neck and instantly sagged against him. "Wow," he commented quietly to Mary Ellen. "That wave of exhaustion hit hard."

"It was a very busy day," she responded gently. "I'm bushwhacked myself."

His eyes locked on hers and she fell into his gaze. "Yeah." Wes shifted on his feet, holding Emma tighter. "Well, I guess we'd better go."

"Let me walk you to the door," Mary Ellen said.

When they got there, Wes gave her a longing look. "Mary Ellen..."

"Yes?"

"I just wanted to say..." His voice sounded rough, like he was battling his emotions. "Thank you."

"You're the one who did me the favor."

"Not entirely. You've helped me remember...certain things that I...haven't thought about in a...long time."

"I didn't do anything special."

"That's just it." He smiled warmly. "All you had to do was be yourself."

Chapter Ten

MARY ELLEN'S HEART was hammering so hard that night she could barely get to sleep. Had Wes meant what she'd thought he had when he'd looked at her in that very soulful way? There was no doubt about it; Mary Ellen was falling for him fast. Was it too much to ask that Wes was equally interested in her? Mary Ellen didn't know what this might mean for her job, or how a relationship with Wes might complicate things. But she couldn't help her burning attraction to him, any more than she could fight her increasing fondness for his precious little girl. By spending the entire day together, they'd bonded in a special way. It wasn't just about building the coop, or getting ice cream... By the time the three of them sat down to dinner, they'd almost felt like a family. The sort of family Mary Ellen had always dreamed about having someday.

Her own upbringing had been so different; with a high-powered mom and no dad in the picture, she'd never enjoyed the familial type of warmth that had shimmered in her kitchen along with the candlelight's comforting glow. Dinner with her mom had been a fast-moving affair, wherein they both ate from take-out containers and Liz studiously surveyed her day planner, reviewing her next day's itinerary. Mary Ellen understood it took all sorts of families to help the world go round, and she had encountered many different arrangements during her teaching. And yet, the type of home environment she'd secretly always yearned for was the type she'd unexpectedly experienced tonight—right here in Sweetheart Valley Hills.

Mary Ellen fluffed her pillow and turned sideways, determined to get some rest. She had a lot of teaching work to catch up on tomorrow, and some errands to run in the afternoon. Meanwhile, she needed her shut-eye, and she hoped that Crazy was resting peacefully, as well. She'd looked in on him at bedtime, and he'd contentedly tucked himself in up on his roost. Maybe Calista Cartwright wasn't going to be a problem after all. Now that Crazy was settled in his new space, in which he had ample room to roam, he'd be less inclined to attempt running away when she took him out of his cage.

***

Mary Ellen woke up at the crack of dawn to a really loud *cock-a-doodle-doo*! She blinked and stared at the ceiling, wondering if she'd had some weird kind of dream. Then the rooster's call sounded again and she remembered... *Crazy!* She sat bolt upright in bed and tossed back the covers. Then, she went bounding through the living room and tearing into the kitchen wearing her pajamas. Mary Ellen paused at the sliding glass door and glanced down at her bare feet, knowing the grass would be freezing cold this early. The sun was just peeking up over the faraway mountains, and tiny icicles clung to the tips of the grass. *Cock-a-doodle-doo!* There he went again! She had to go and grab him before Mrs. Cartwright came barreling through the back gate!

Mary Ellen hurriedly unlatched the door then slid it open, scurrying across the frigid stone patio and onto the frost-covered lawn, which—*yikes!*—was even colder than she'd expected. Chill bumps raced up her legs as she dashed toward Crazy's cage. He stood proud and tall inside it, letting out his morning charge like the wailer on a minaret!

"*Crazy,*" she said in hushed tones. "*Shush!*"

He blinked and took two giant steps backwards, clawing at the earth. As he positioned himself to crow again, Mary Ellen flung open the coop door. She grabbed for him, but he scuttled out of reach. She tried again, and he deftly avoided her grasp. Then, to her horror, Mary Ellen experienced a huge fluttering of wings right up near her face. She gasped and sprang back as Crazy shot straight out of his cage. He made it to the fence before she could stop him. Next, he hopped right up on it, then flew down into the front yard, waddling toward the street.

Mary Ellen gasped and raced after him, taking the closest exit at the side gate. Thank goodness, the street was quiet with most of her neighbors still sleeping. All of them except...

"Good morning, Mary Ellen."

She snapped to attention to find Wes standing practically in front of her, dressed in a sweatshirt and jeans. He was holding his morning paper and Crazy had perched at his feet. Wes bent low and picked up the rooster. His brow rose with amusement. "Lose something?"

"I was trying to...get him to stop crowing." Mary Ellen struggled to catch her breath as her icy toes grew numb.

Wes viewed her feet with concern. "You should at least have put some slippers on."

"I know! There wasn't...time."

"What's your hurry?"

"Mrs. Cartwright," she hissed frantically. "She said, if I had a chicken, she'd turn me in!"

"Turn you in?" Wes screwed up his face. "To whom?"

"The neighborhood association police."

"I see."

"I can't lose my rental already," she pleaded with panic in her eyes. "I've paid two months in advance!"

Wes jostled the bird in his arms and carefully handed him to Mary Ellen. "What's Mrs. Cartwright's complaint?"

"Something about farm animals in the city."

"Yeah. There's that. I was hoping it wouldn't be a problem." Wes frowned sympathetically. "I suppose some neighbors are less tolerant than others."

Mary Ellen viewed him desperately. "What am I going to do? I can't give Crazy away! Something bad might happen to him..."

"Like?"

"I'm not going to even mention Colonel Sanders."

"Right." He glanced compassionately at the bird. "Crazy and I will pretend we didn't hear that."

"Wes?" she scanned his eyes, searching for answers.

"Don't worry," he told her firmly. "We'll think of something."

"And in the meantime?"

"You could try covering his coop at night, with something dark like a tarp." Wes thoughtfully stroked his chin. "Or even bringing him indoors first thing in the morning."

"At *dawn*?"

"Only temporarily," Wes tried to assure her. "Until we can find a better solution."

***

Wes wished he hadn't promised Mary Ellen he'd help solve her Crazy problem, because now he was unsure of how to do that. She'd dropped by his office and confided that she'd begun a new routine of having Crazy sleep indoors, then spend his daylight hours outdoors while she was at work. The only trouble was,

Crazy appeared to like his coop better than being inside. While his inside cage had suited him before, he no longer wanted to tolerate it. He screeched and wildly flapped his wings while clawing at the cage floor, and the moment she released him from his nighttime prison, he raced to the back door. Crazy seemed to like being outside. It was apparently a lot more entertaining to peck at the dirt, where he might unearth worms or tiny bugs, rather than to forage for fun at the base of a wire cage lined with newspaper.

While he hadn't foreseen this complication, Wes felt partially responsible for Mary Ellen's worries. He was the one who'd suggested building the coop to begin with. Although he'd thought it would be better for the rooster, he hadn't known a nosy neighbor had threatened to turn the hapless pet into chicken fricassee.

At least Emma's unicorn project had been a success. Upon reflection and study, he and his little girl had arrived at the answers to the teacher's three questions, and Emma had diligently produced a delightful three-paneled drawing. The first showed a sleeping girl with a dream bubble above her bed. In it, a tiny unicorn hovered on a cloud. This meant, unicorns came from our dreams. Emma decided that since unicorns were horse-like they should enjoy horse-like treats. But unicorns were extra sweet! So, she showed her unicorn eating a candy apple. Finally, she drew a bed of straw for her unicorn, but rather than being in a barn stall, it was placed in a garage—right beside a lawn mower. Wes had chuckled at this, imagining his surprise at encountering such a mythical creature on his way to cut the grass.

In any case, Miss Meeks had given Emma high marks on the assignment, and she'd been equally rewarding to the rest of her class. According to her teaching assistant, Mary Ellen had a way of bringing out the best in her students and Wes certainly believed it. She clearly had inspired some sort of change in him. Ever since Saturday, Wes hadn't been able to stop thinking about her. It didn't help that he had regular opportunities to pass by her room on his way to the cafeteria. He also received nightly reports from Emma about what she was learning in school. The most amazingly wonderful thing about it was how much fun Emma appeared to be having. Mary Ellen had a special way with her teaching that made her lessons come alive and the children want to please her. Even the wiggly little boys had learned to sit still when Miss Meeks gave her signal.

Wes couldn't help but think about what a really great mother Mary Ellen would make. In general of course. And, down the road. For somebody else's children entirely. Wes already had a delightful little girl. Once he'd lost Patricia, he'd believed that the fates had sent him a very clear sign. One perfectly angelic child was all Wes was meant to have. And, up until now, that had obviously been enough. Only lately, Wes had found himself secretly wondering how Emma might react to having a baby brother or sister. She was such a nurturing child, Wes had to guess she'd love being able to cuddle and eventually mentor a younger sibling. Just as he'd done with Jenny. Right. And just look how that turned out! With Jenny bossing him around!

She'd called three times this week to inquire about his relationship with the pretty blonde he'd brought by Cherry on Top. Jenny highly approved of the fact that Mary Ellen was a neighbor, and couldn't see any conflict of interest at all relating to Wes being her boss. *Come on, bro*, she'd ribbed lightly. *You've got to know it happens all the time! A supervisor falling for his protégé!* Wes straightened his tie, thinking maybe it did. But that didn't mean it had to happen to him. How would that look at the school? Then, he'd have Central Office to answer to! None of that knowledge kept him from privately wanting to spend more time with Mary Ellen, however. Emma was anxious to see her again outside of school, too. She'd been pestering her daddy about inviting Mary Ellen to their house, because it was their turn, according to Emma. Since Miss Meeks had already had them over!

Someone knocked at his door and Wes looked up to find Mary Ellen standing on the threshold. "Tina said you wanted to see me during my planning time?" she asked with a blush.

Wes uncertainly cleared his throat. "Yes, please. Come in."

She did and sat in a chair. "Is this about...school?"

"No, not exactly," Wes hedged, gathering his nerve. He'd been trying to think up another way to see her. An excuse that seemed casual and totally aboveboard. "I just wanted to ask your advice about...something."

Her pretty blue eyes rounded. "Yes?"

"It's about Emma," he said, lowering his voice.

"Emma?" Mary Ellen appeared startled. "I hope she's all right! Just this morning she seemed—"

"Oh, no. It's nothing like that," he said, stopping her quickly. "It's about Halloween."

"Halloween?" Mary Ellen appeared taken aback. "I'm not sure I follow."

"It's about her costume." Wes leaned forward in his seat. "She wants to be a princess."

Mary Ellen smiled broadly, her face awash with relief. "Is that all? Well, I'm sure you can find plenty of princess costumes at the—"

"I'm afraid this one has to be homemade," he said, deadpan, and Mary Ellen's brow rose.

"Oh?"

Wes flattened his palms on his desk. "She wants to be a very special kind of princess," he whispered conspiratorially. "A *unicorn* princess. I have no idea where to find an outfit like that. I've looked online, but it somehow seems very specific."

Mary Ellen grinned in understanding. "You're asking for my help, aren't you?"

"I wouldn't if I weren't desperate. Halloween's less than a week away."

"And you think this has something to do with my assignment," Mary Ellen surmised.

"It might. I...I'm not sure." Mary Ellen surveyed him quietly but Wes could tell that she was thinking about it. "I hear you're very good," he said, laying it on thick. "An excellent seamstress. Tina says you're making all the kindergarten costumes for the Thanksgiving play."

"I am pretty good with a needle and thread," she said proudly. "Give me a sewing machine with a bobbin and I do even better."

"Do you need one?" he asked, fearing his desperation was way too apparent.

"I already own one." She smiled saucily and his heart stilled. "But thanks for the thought."

"So, you'll do it? Help make Emma's costume? I'll pay for the materials, of course. And also for your time," he said a bit unsurely. "I don't know what a seamstress would normally—"

"I don't want you to pay me in money," she said boldly and Wes's skin burned hot.

Her face softened in a smile. "Dinner with you and Emma will do just fine."

"Only under one condition," Wes countered quickly.

"Yeah? What's that?"

"That you'll join us afterwards when we go trick-or-treating?" He shot her a petitioning look then added warmly, "Emma would really love that." After a beat, he added hoarsely, "I'd really like it, too."

Mary Ellen grinned brightly. "So would I."

Chapter Eleven

ON HALLOWEEN EVENING, Emma pivoted proudly in front of her bedroom dresser mirror. The pink and purple organza skirt of her long princess dress fanned out around her as she turned happily toward Mary Ellen. "It's so pretty!"

"You look gorgeous," Wes commented from nearby. The gown had a sparkly bodice with a smiling unicorn appliqué on the front. The puffy pink and purple cap sleeves complemented the colors in the skirt that also streamed with glittery gold and silver ribbons.

"Your tiara," Mary Ellen said, gently placing the small plastic crown on Emma's head.

Emma beamed delightedly when Mary Ellen handed her a wand next. Mary Ellen had ordered the toy tiara and matching wand online, then modified the wand with streamers to match the ones on Emma's hand-sewn dress.

"I believe you're the prettiest Unicorn Princess I've ever seen." Mary Ellen stepped back to admire the glowing child, and Wes whispered from behind her.

"Likely, the *only* Unicorn Princess you've seen."

Mary Ellen shushed him quietly and adjusted Emma's crown. "Why don't you let me slip in a few bobby pins to hold it steady?" she suggested tenderly. "We can't have your tiara tumbling off into your plastic jack o'lantern!"

Emma giggled at the thought. "No, my pumpkin is for candy."

"Remember, we're going to wait to eat it when we get home." Wes patted Emma's shoulder as he issued his reminder and she rolled her big green eyes.

"I *know*, Daddy." Emma looked up at Mary Ellen. "Daddy has to check the candy first."

"A very good idea," Mary Ellen agreed. "My mom always checked—" She stopped herself abruptly, feeling as if she'd made a misstep. The last thing she should have done was mention mothers on an evening when so many neighborhood kids were out with theirs, and Emma didn't have one. "What I mean is, if I'd had a daddy as great as yours, I'd have wanted him to check my candy, too."

Emma's brow furrowed. "Where did your daddy go?"

"Honestly, sweetie?" Mary Ellen's heart pinged at the admission. "I just don't know."

Wes gallantly stepped in to smooth things over. "Families come in all shapes and sizes. Emma and I have talked about that." He fondly glanced at his daughter before continuing. "The important thing is knowing that you're cared for and you belong."

"Like I belong to you, Daddy." Emma smiled broadly and Mary Ellen's heart melted.

"You have a wonderful daddy," she told the little girl. "You're very lucky."

Emma paused in thought. After a moment she asked Wes, "Can you be Miss Meeks's daddy, too?"

Wes flushed, taken aback. "Her dad...? Well, no. I don't suppose that would work, actually."

"Why not?" Emma asked innocently.

Mary Ellen's cheeks heated as she answered, "Your daddy and I are practically the same age, for one thing."

Emma's small lips turned down in a frown. "How old are you?" she asked Mary Ellen.

"I'm...er...twenty-seven."

The girl stared expectantly at Wes next and he awkwardly cleared his throat. "Thirty-four, but it hardly matt—"

"But Miss Meeks just said that it did?" Emma asked, perplexed.

"I think what your dad's trying to say," Mary Ellen began sweetly, "is that, even though he and I are both adults, your daddy's not enough older than me to be *my* dad." Her brow crinkled as she queried, "Does that make sense?"

Emma lowered her wand and pursed her lips. "I guess," she said after a bit, but she sounded very disappointed. Seconds later, her face brightened with a new idea. "Maybe you can be my mommy?"

Wes coughed so loudly at this, Mary Ellen had to pat him on the back. "Oh, look! The sun is going down," he quickly said, glancing out Emma's bedroom window. "Looks like we'd better get ready for trick-or-treating. We'll need to set our bowl of candy out on the porch, along with the sign we—"

"Why can't she?" Emma asked Wes, stopping him mid-stride.

"Well, I..." He swallowed hard then ran a hand through his hair.

"Is Miss Meeks too old?"

"Old? No," Wes said, flummoxed.

"Too young?" Emma's eyes widened and Wes blinked hard.

"No, not too young at all." Mary Ellen had the sense Wes was trying really, really hard not to look at her. "Miss Meeks is at a great age! Really perfect!"

Emma beamed at them both, then bounced up and down excitedly. "Yippee!" She sprang at her daddy's legs, wrapping her tiny arms around them.

Wes blanched as he glanced down, then over at Mary Ellen. "What have I just done?" he whispered hoarsely.

Mary Ellen grimaced, her heart pounding. "I think you've just agreed."

"What?"

Emma raced to hug Mary Ellen next, and Mary Ellen stooped to catch her in her arms. "Can I call you Mommy, now?" she asked, hugging Mary Ellen's neck tightly.

"Sweetie, I... Er... Um..." Mary Ellen stared helplessly up at Wes, who appeared as lost as she was. Actually, probably a lot more.

"Emma," Wes said gently. He laid his hand tenderly on his daughter's back. "I'm afraid that's not how things work, sweetheart."

Emma released Mary Ellen and surveyed her father with a heart-wrenching frown.

"For someone to become your mommy, I'd have to marry them. Just like I married your real mom, Patricia, back before you were born."

Emma stewed on this, then uttered a disconsolate, "Oh."

"And I'm not..." Wes twisted the wedding band on his finger, purposely avoiding Mary Ellen's gaze. "Planning on marrying again anytime soon."

Emma puffed out her bottom lip. "Well, it's not a bad idea."

Mary Ellen gently stroked the little girl's hair. "I'm very flattered, Emma. Thank you. Flattered that you'd like me to be your...sister...or...uh...mom. But, right now, your dad's and my lives are so busy—"

"Okay," Emma said with a sigh. Then she petitioned them both with a worried look. "But can we still go trick-or-treating? Puhleeze?"

"Of course we can," Wes said, wrapping his arms around her. "And we're going to have the best time, aren't we, Miss Meeks?"

Mary Ellen plastered on her brightest smile. "You bet! Let the trick-or-treating begin!"

***

Wes's pulse pounded so loudly in his ears, he could barely hear himself think. After getting Emma out the door, they'd managed several successful rounds of trick-or-treating as they circled around the various streets of the neighborhood. Everyone got that Emma was a princess, but not everyone guessed that she was a Unicorn Princess, until the child politely corrected them. When they unexpectedly arrived at Calista Cartwright's door, she greeted the trio with a startled look.

"It's you!"

"Happy Halloween, Mrs. Cartwright," Mary Ellen said cordially.

Mrs. Cartwright held her candy bowl in Emma's direction, complimenting the child on her costume.

"Miss Meeks made it!" Emma informed the older woman.

Mrs. Cartwright viewed Mary Ellen with surprise, then carefully studied the child. "Well, I must say it's very lovely. Nice work!" she told Mary Ellen, who smiled at the comment.

"Thank you."

"I'm Wes Johnson," Wes said, holding out his hand. "I don't believe we've properly met."

"Calista Cartwright," she said primly, as she accepted his handshake.

"And, this is my daughter, Emma," Wes continued. "I believe you've already met our neighbor, Mary Ellen Meeks."

Calista slightly narrowed her eyes. "Yes, we met the other day."

"I hope things have been quiet enough for you," Mary Ellen offered.

Calista suspiciously twisted her lips, then said, "There've been no more complaints."

"That's excellent, then," Wes said, clapping his hands together. He glanced over his shoulder, seeing a band of older children in costume bounding up Calista's front walk. "I guess we'd better make room for the others." Wes nodded at the older woman. "It was very nice meeting you."

As he and Mary Ellen trailed Emma, who was on a trajectory to the next house, Wes whispered to Mary Ellen, "Seems like that problem is solved."

But, rather than appearing relieved, she just bit her bottom lip. "Hope so."

***

Later that night, after sorting Emma's candy and letting her select a few choice pieces to try, Wes helped Emma brush her teeth and tucked her into bed. She'd said goodnight to Mary Ellen downstairs, after giving her a big hug and thanking her again for the pretty costume. Wes had asked Mary Ellen to stay and have a cup of hot cider with him on the front porch, and he was glad she'd agreed. He couldn't let that awkwardness about Emma wanting Mary Ellen to be her mommy linger between them. It would be best to discuss things openly and clear the air.

He returned to his living area to find Mary Ellen flipping through one of the magazines on his coffee table. As he descended the stairs, she looked up and smiled. "Everything go okay up there?"

"Oh yeah, just fine. Emma went out like a light the moment her head hit the pillow. I think she was asleep before I was out the door."

Mary Ellen chuckled sweetly at this. "She did have a very full day."

"And an even busier evening, it's true." When Mary Ellen closed the magazine in her hand and set it back on the coffee table, Wes asked her, "Would you still like that cider?"

"I'd love some," she said, standing and following him into the kitchen. Wes's house was homey and tastefully done, thanks in large part to the nice finishing touches that Patricia had put on it when they moved in. "I really like your house," Mary Ellen said, glancing around the comfy kitchen with a big farm table and hanging rows of copper pots and pans above the granite countertops.

"Patricia gets most of the credit," he said honestly. "Other than basic repairs to the roof and so on, I haven't done much to it. Besides replace all the windows," he added, motioning to the one above the kitchen sink.

"Well, everything looks in really great shape. A lot better than my place," she said with a laugh.

Wes shrugged and pulled the jug of cider from his refrigerator. "Your place is a rental."

"True."

He filled their mugs and popped them in the microwave. "Thank you again for Emma's costume."

"She already thanked me herself a dozen times." Mary Ellen grinned warmly. "You've raised your daughter with very good manners."

"It would be unseemly for the principal's daughter to have bad ones."

Mary Ellen's grin broadened. "You're very good at what you do, you know that? And, I'm not just talking about at school. You do a great job around here, too."

"I'd say you're equally talented." The microwave beeped and he handed her a mug. "You're a lot more talented that I imagined, in fact. Who knew you were so good at sewing? Not to mention a very fine rooster mother."

Her cheeks colored sweetly. "Wes, about Emma—"

"Yeah, we need to discuss that, but why don't we wait until we get outside? It's a bit chilly now that it's gotten later. Are you sure you still want to sit on the porch?"

"We can put our jackets on."

"Great thought." He led them back into the living room and grabbed their jackets from his coat closet, handing Mary Ellen hers. Once they'd both slipped into them, Wes held back the door and they carried their cider onto the front porch.

The night air was nippy and crisp, with a light breeze rustling through the brittle leaves on the trees.

The young trick-or-treaters had all turned in, but several jack o'lanterns still glowed on porch stoops, casting flickering shadows toward the street.

When they each took a seat in a rocker, Wes began, "Mary Ellen, about Emma and what she said—"

"It's all right, Wes," Mary Ellen replied kindly. "You really don't have to explain." There was warmth in her pretty blue eyes as she continued. "I've been around little kids a lot. Certainly enough to know that they generally speak in innocence, and often from the heart."

He viewed her in the soft light, thinking about how pretty she was, inside and out. "You're being really gracious about this."

She took a sip of her cider, saying how good it was. Then her eyes settled on his. "How long has it been?" she asked gently. "Since Patricia—?"

"Two and a half years."

"So, Emma doesn't really remember?"

"Not much," Wes said with a touch of melancholy. "Only a few things."

"Like?"

"She recalls her mom's beautiful singing voice."

"I'm sure it was lovely." She paused and then added, "I'll bet Patricia was, too."

"What makes you say that?" Wes viewed her in the shadows and Mary Ellen smiled softly.

"She was married to you, and also Emma's mother. Both those things say a lot."

The back of Wes's neck heated as he felt moved by Mary Ellen's words. "Thank you," he said hoarsely. "I mean it. Thanks a lot for saying that."

Mary Ellen met his eyes. "You're a good man, Wes. And, a great catch, if I'm being honest. I know now's not the time, but if—and when—you decide you're ready for a new mommy for Emma, I don't think you'll have any trouble finding one."

Wes thoughtfully sipped from his mug before asking, "How about you? I mean, I realize you're not very old."

"But too old to be your daughter!" she teased with a laugh, and Wes laughed with her.

"Yeah. That much is true."

She studied him over the rim of her mug. "You were saying?"

"Asking was really more like it, and you can tell me it's none of my business if you want..."

"Go on?"

"I was just wondering why someone so...pretty..." He stumbled a bit on the word, hoping he wasn't sounding overly forward. "And available hasn't been snatched up already?"

"Oh, I was," she answered surely. "Snatched up." Her expression turned from sunny to downcast. "But that was right before I was let down."

"I'm sorry, Mary Ellen."

"I was moving to Boston to be with my boyfriend. He'd hinted at marriage, though he'd never exactly said anything concrete."

"No proposal?" Wes asked, astounded. "No ring?"

She dourly shook her head. "I'm afraid not."

"His loss is going to be another man's gain," Wes said, before he could stop himself. "Someday."

Moisture sparkled in Mary Ellen's eyes. "That's very sweet, Wes. Thank you."

He'd meant it, though, so he wasn't backing down. "It's true, Mary Ellen, and very obvious. At least, it's patently obvious to me. You're a kind, generous-hearted woman, who's skilled at her job and has a way with kids." He was about to mention her stellar looks again, but then thought better of it, lest she think he was hitting on her. "Any guy—any rational man—could see that. Your ex was foolish to let you get away."

"He said he wanted someone more accomplished." The hurt in her voice shone through.

"What made him so important and judgmental?"

"I'm not sure," she said sadly. "I suppose that's just who he was."

"Then you're better off without him."

"Yes," she said decidedly. "I believe that I am. Though I didn't in the beginning."

"What do you mean?"

"The break-up hit me hard. I'd already resigned from my teaching position in preparation for the move."

"Oh wow, I'm sorry. Did you have a job lined up in Boston?"

"No, I intended to look when I got there, and substitute teach while applying for a more permanent position."

"Then your mom's illness hit," Wes said sympathetically. "How awful that must have been—"

"Wes," she said stopping him. He was surprised by the serious expression in her eyes. "I need to tell you something about my mother."

"What is it?" he asked with concern. "What's wrong?"

"Nothing is wrong with Liz. Nothing at all."

"She's not sick?"

Mary Ellen shook her head. "Never has been."

Wes was completely thrown by this admission. "I'm not sure I get what you're telling me?"

"That time off that I took?" Her lower lip trembled and Wes resisted the urge to reach for her hand. "It wasn't to help anyone but myself."

"But your former principal said—"

"It was all a horrible misunderstanding," she answered with a sniff. "I never told anyone I was going to care for my ill mother. I only confided in a few coworkers that my mom was taking *me* to a health retreat, and somehow things got twisted around. I didn't want to tell anyone that Jeff had dumped me. The school had given me a big going-away party, and I couldn't bear to lose face. Pride goes before the fall, I guess."

Her eyes glistened, and Wes's heart ached for her. "You must think I'm a horrible person to have let that rumor stand. But I thought it was..." she sucked in a gasp, fighting back her tears. "*Personal...*" Mary Ellen set down her mug and covered her mouth with her hand. When she spoke again, her voice cracked. "I never even dreamed something about my mom being sick would land in my professional file." She sent him a sad, petitioning look. "I mean, how did that even happen?"

"I don't know." Wes viewed her kindly. "But I do know this. It sounds like an honest mix-up, not like something that was your fault."

Fear and worry registered in her moist blue eyes. "Am I going to lose my job here?"

"Lose it? No. Why?" He observed her reassuringly. "Mary Ellen, listen to me. You're an excellent teacher, who came highly credentialed. Plus, you're already proving yourself on the job. You couldn't help what was written in a recommendation letter about you. It's not like you claimed to be Florence Nightingale on your resume."

This brought a smile, albeit a shaky one. "You're being very kind."

"I've meant every word."

She picked her cider back up and took another sip. "Well, thanks," she said, finally appearing to relax. "Thanks for understanding."

Wes studied her, a question forming in his mind. "So, if you weren't caring for your sick mother during your hiatus from teaching, what were you doing?"

"Well, I was *staying* with my mom," Mary Ellen said, sounding and appearing more composed. "But she was absolutely caring for herself. In the meantime..." She appeared completely abashed by what she was about to say next. "I was writing...poetry."

"Poetry?" Wes asked, astounded. His brow shot up. "Was it any good?"

"Frankly? It was dreadful." Mary Ellen giggled and her candor warmed his soul.

"I bet it wasn't as bad as you think."

"Oh yes, it was," she said, grinning.

Wes grinned back. "You're a very interesting woman, Miss Meeks."

"Oh yeah?" She cocked an eyebrow and Wes's heart stuttered. "Well, I find you pretty interesting, too, *Mr. Johnson.*"

Chapter Twelve

IT WAS IMPOSSIBLE for Wes to focus on his job back at school. He knew he was supposed to be working with the planning team on the revised curriculum, but all he could think of was seeing Mary Ellen. And not *seeing*, as in catching a glimpse of her each time he strode by her classroom "accidentally on purpose" about fifty times each day. He wanted to date her, and see where that might lead. The notion had hit him like a thunderbolt, as he'd watched her cross the cul-de-sac when she'd headed home on Halloween night. He'd felt an odd burning in his chest as he'd watched her walk away. Wes hadn't wanted her to go so soon. He'd ached to spend more time with her, and learn more about her. Hear about the places she'd been and the things she'd seen. Wes yearned to share things about himself, too, and have Mary Ellen accept him—and Emma—as two very special people in her life.

The three of them fit together so well, almost like a real family. Maybe if they gave it time, this budding bond between them would continue to grow. Wes didn't care that he was the principal and that Mary Ellen was his teacher. At the same time, he wasn't so selfish that he'd cause her to risk losing her job. The truth was, Wes couldn't afford to lose his either. He was good at what he did and he needed the income to provide for Emma. Perhaps someday in the future, he'd also be providing, at least in part, for a new wife. Wes had never been able to imagine he'd remarry again, but that had been before he'd started secretly wondering what it might be like having Mary Ellen as his wife.

Wes was unsure of what to do and how to handle things. He'd been through the county personnel manual a dozen times and hadn't found anything expressly prohibiting two school coworkers from dating or marrying. The gray area came in because he was Mary Ellen's supervisor. So, if he made a move on her that could be seen as improper at best. And, at worse, as workplace harassment. To add an additional complication to the mix, Mary Ellen was also Emma's teacher. Wes sighed heavily and ran a hand through his hair.

He was still puzzling things out when Mary Ellen appeared at his office door, looking shattered.

"Mary Ellen?" Wes asked with alarm. "What is it? What's wrong?"

Her eyes were red-rimmed and she appeared on the verge of tears. "It's Crazy," she told him. "A man came from Animal Control this morning and took him away."

***

Wes asked Becky to schedule a substitute for the afternoon, so Mary Ellen could go to the SPCA. He rearranged his appointments so he could go with her, calculating that—if they left the school at noon—he could be home in plenty of time to meet Emma's bus. However, when he and Mary Ellen arrived at the animal shelter, they were greeted with bad news.

"I'm afraid your rooster's gone," the woman sitting behind the front desk said. She was in her mid-thirties and slim with a pleasant looking face and shoulder-length red hair. Beyond her, Wes spied a separate room lined with cat cages. Another door led to an area populated with dog runs.

Mary Ellen stared back at the woman in shock. "Gone? But, how? He was just picked up this morning?"

The woman double-checked her computer screen against some paperwork on her desk. "I'm sorry, ma'am, I really am. Generally roosters aren't scooped up so quickly, but it appears yours has already been adopted."

"Adopted?" Wes asked, dismayed.

The shelter worker shrugged helplessly. "It seems someone needed him to help calm their hens."

"But, Crazy is a house pet!" Mary Ellen protested. "Well, it's true he's been in the yard *lately*. But I still bring him inside! Every night!"

"Can't you at least tell us where he's been taken?" Wes asked reasonably. "Perhaps, if we talk to his new family, they'll realize this has been a mistake."

The lady sadly shook her head. "I'm afraid that's against regulations. All adoptions here are confidential."

Mary Ellen's shoulders sagged in exasperated disbelief. "It had to have been Mrs. Cartwright," she said to Wes. "I can't think of anyone else who might have turned me in."

Wes beheld her worriedly. "I'm so sorry, Mary Ellen."

She fretfully met his eyes. "Emma's going to miss him, too."

"I know. She was begging me for another rooster play date just this morning." The moment the words were out of his mouth, Wes regretted them, because they caused Mary Ellen to burst into sobs.

Without thinking, he took her in his arms. "We'll get Crazy back," he said, holding her firmly. "We'll find a way."

Mary Ellen stared up at him, her eyes teary. "Yes, but how?"

***

Later that afternoon, when Emma was at a friend's house, Wes decided to pay a visit to Mrs. Cartwright.

"Mr. Johnson! Oh! This is a surprise," she said, appearing befuddled.

"I'm afraid this isn't a social call," Wes returned solemnly. "I'm here about a certain rooster."

"Rooster? Heavens! I have no idea what you mean," she answered, all the while looking like she did.

"My friend, Mary Ellen, had a pet one, but now it seems it's been taken away."

"Well, good rid—" She abruptly cupped a hand over her mouth. "What I meant was—"

"Did you call Animal Control this morning?"

"Well, I..." Mrs. Cartwright adjusted the fit of her bulky wool jacket. "Had to! Can't you see?" Her eyebrows arched. "It was a patent violation! Intolerable! A farm animal, can you imagine? Chickens are so filthy!"

"Are they?" Wes asked sadly. "That's funny. I thought I'd heard something else."

"Oh?" Mrs. Cartwright challenged. "What's that?"

"That they're very loving."

"A rooster? Hoo!" She sniggled dismissively. "And, where were you raised, Mr. Johnson? On a farm?"

He studied the woman a long while before answering. "Actually, Mrs. Cartwright... Yes. Yes, I was." He held out his hand and she took it reluctantly.

"What are you doing?"

Wes gave her hand a firm squeeze. "Saying thank you."

"Thanking me? For what?"

"Helping me get my head on straight."

As he departed Mrs. Cartwright's stoop, Wes noted a new spring in his step. Even though it had some wonderful aspects, he'd never felt quite at home in this suburban neighborhood. His conversation with Mrs. Cartwright had underscored why. Wes wasn't meant to live in the city. Not when he was a country boy at heart.

Chapter Thirteen

THAT EVENING, WES took Emma to visit his folks downtown. While she helped her grandma bake cookies in the kitchen, Wes had a man-to-man chat with his dad.

Wes's father, Luke, had a similar build but silvery hair and gray eyes. The green eyes had come from Wes's mother, Jill. "I have to say this is a surprise," Luke told him. "A pleasant one, but still, it's unexpected." Wes had just told him what his parents had long wanted to hear: that he was interested in moving into the family farmhouse, Misty Meadows. "Does Emma know about this?"

"No," Wes said honestly. "But I hardly think she'd be opposed. Fresh air...wide open spaces...room for animals to roam. Plus, her Aunt Jenny and Uncle Ian will be right next door."

"Yes, that's a perk," Luke answered. "I'm just a little stunned by the turnaround. Last time we talked you said you could never leave your current house. It's where you lived with Patricia and built all those memories."

"That's true," Wes answered seriously. "But sometimes it's good to think about making new memories. Besides, I've got plenty of fond memories of growing up at Misty Meadows. I've always thought it would be nice for Emma to enjoy that sort of life."

"It's not a very far commute to your school," his dad commented. "Misty Meadows is to the west of the town."

"Yes, it's convenient."

"And, the timing is right," his dad said with a twinkle. "The current renters are leaving next month."

"That's what I'd heard. I'd just never considered moving until now."

"What changed your mind?"

"It's kind of crazy..." Wes shook his head with a chuckle. "What I mean is, it really was Crazy..."

"Boy, I'm not sure you're making any sense." Luke's gaze snagged on Wes's bare wedding ring finger and his eyebrows rose. "You've put Patricia's ring away?"

"I decided it was time."

"Does this have to do with a woman?" his dad asked appraisingly.

Wes met his dad's gaze dead-on. "It might."

"What makes you think this gal would be keen on Misty Meadows?"

"She's got a rooster for a pet!"

Luke laughed out loud before Wes's serious expression silenced him. "I mean, *had* a rooster. We're going to have to work on that. Finding him, I mean."

"This is all sounding very involved," Luke remarked. "I suppose that Emma likes her?"

"Emma loves her. She's Emma's kindergarten teacher, and a very good one."

"Well, it won't be the first time. Will it?"

"The first time for what?" Wes asked, surprised.

"Two people falling for each other on the job." Luke smiled in recollection. "When I met your mother, I was working for her. She was bookkeeping at the Smiths' dairy and I was a hired hand."

"Dad, I—"

"I know times have changed," Luke went on. "And that you can't overstep any lines at school. But, son?"

Wes waited while his dad continued.

"If you truly care for this woman, then you have to go with your gut. And, listen to your heart."

"I don't want to cause trouble for her—or me—at Turtle Creek Elementary."

"You tread lightly then," his dad advised. "If she's really interested, she'll find a way to let you know."

"And, if she's not?"

"Will you still want the farm?"

"Yes," Wes said firmly. "I've decided that I do. That's where I have my roots, and where I came from. I want Emma to experience that sense of having a homestead, too."

"Then, talk to your daughter and tell her the good news," Luke said. "Meanwhile, I'll remove the rental listing from the internet."

At that moment, Emma barreled into the room holding a cookie on a napkin. "Poppy, look! I made one just for you!"

"Delightful!" he said, smiling warmly at Emma. He pulled the child onto his lap and snuggled her close, admiring the cookie. "Thank you!" Before he took it from her to take a bite, Luke held his hand up toward Wes with two fingers crossed. "And on that other matter..." Luke winked confidentially at his son. "Good luck!"

***

The next morning, Emma surprised Mary Ellen with a bit of news at show-and-tell time.

"We're moving to the farm!"

Mary Ellen's eyes were still red from crying herself to sleep last night over losing Crazy. Now, she felt like she wanted to burst into tears again. But, she couldn't do that! That's precisely what had happened with the previous teacher, Ms. Cantor. She'd totally lost it in front of the class.

"What do you mean, sweetie?" she asked Emma just as calmly as she could.

"Daddy and I are going to live at Misty Meadows! It's so cool there! You can come visit, and bring Crazy!"

Mary Ellen stifled a sob when she realized that Wes hadn't told Emma about Crazy being gone. Perhaps he was hoping against hope that Mary Ellen would get her rooster back, so Emma wouldn't have to know he'd been taken away. "That's so sweet, honey," Mary Ellen managed.

Tina noted her fragile state and burst in merrily, "Who'd like to sing 'Old McDonald'?"

Tons of tiny hands shot up, and Tina whispered to Mary Ellen, "Go on and take a breather. I'll manage."

Mary Ellen nodded and excused herself from the room. When she stepped into the hall, her whole world crumbled. She'd come to Paradise for a new beginning at this great new school, and then she'd found it. What was more, she'd found herself growing helplessly attracted to her new boss. Wes must have felt it, too. And, this apparently had created problems. Now, they were leaving! *Leaving*...Wes and Emma, both. Mary Ellen recalled Wes mentioning that his parents owned a farm, but she had no idea exactly where it was located.

She hoped it wasn't so far away that Emma would be changing schools. The thought that Wes might be abandoning his post as principal was devastating, too. But, no, he wouldn't do that. Wes had a solid job here, and personal ties to Turtle Creek Elementary. He'd gone here himself as a child, and surely would want Emma to continue her education here as well. Mary Ellen slumped back against the wall, her head and heart reeling. Whether or not she continued to see Wes and Emma at work, not having them across the street would be sure to impact their friendship. She no longer even had a matchmaking rooster to give her and Wes's fledgling relationship a boost. And it *had been* going somewhere. Whether or not she and Wes had discussed it openly, she'd sensed it with every fiber of her being.

"Everything okay, Miss Meeks?" Mary Ellen's head jerked up and she saw Wes standing before her. He'd apparently been on his way to the cafeteria, which was a route he appeared to be taking a lot these days. Mary Ellen suspected it was because those fifth graders were getting out of control again, but she wasn't entirely sure. She couldn't dare to hope that Wes kept passing by her classroom merely with the hope of seeing her.

"I...uh...heard you and Emma are moving?"

"That's right," he replied steadily. "Sometime next month." Wes shared a warm smile. "We won't be going far, though. Less than fifteen miles away."

"Oh! Then you won't...?"

"Emma will remain at Turtle Creek Elementary." His green eyes sparkled. "So will I."

Mary Ellen drew in a breath, trying not to let her emotions show, even though they felt raw and obvious. "Well, that's good then! Much better for Emma, I'm sure."

"Better for everyone." He scrutinized her a beat and Mary Ellen's heart pounded. "I hope?"

"Yes," she said breathlessly. "Uh-huh."

"You look a little pale." He viewed her with concern. "Do you think you should see the nurse?"

"Er...maybe," Mary Ellen hedged, thinking that a sick day sounded good. If she hadn't taken part of the day off yesterday to try to track down Crazy, she might be tempted to take a personal day to sort things. She felt so confused and extremely conflicted. While she naturally wanted what was best for Wes and Emma, her heart broke at the thought of them leaving Sweetheart Valley Hills. At the moment, they were the only friends she had there, not counting Calista Cartwright. And Mary Ellen definitely *didn't* count her.

"Why don't you go and let her take your temperature?" he suggested kindly. "Check your pulse?"

There was no need for that. It was beating double-time just because Wes was looking in her eyes. "Wes...I, I mean, I'm sorry. Mr. Johnson—"

"Yes?"

"Forgive me. I'm still so thrown over the whole situation with Crazy."

"Of course you are. It was unthinkable of Mrs. Cartwright to do that."

"How can you be so sure it was her?"

"I paid Calista a little visit."

Mary Ellen stared at him in shock. "And?"

"She didn't admit things outright, but close enough, anyhow. Sadly, I'm not sure she's the least bit sorry." He locked on her gaze. "But I am, Miss Meeks. I mean it. And, I still want to help if I can."

"I'm not sure how," she said lamely. "The woman at the shelter made it seem like a lost cause."

"Maybe you'd like another rooster?" he ventured.

"I'm not sure anyone could take Crazy's place."

"I hear what you're saying." Wes share a wan smile. "Crazy seemed to like us both, and he took a special shine to Emma."

"Yeah."

A fifth grade teacher emerged in the hall, leading her class toward the cafeteria. "I suppose that's my cue to go," Wes said, glancing that way. "Have a good rest of your day, Miss Meeks."

"Thanks, Mr. Johnson. You, too."

***

Mary Ellen wasn't sure how she did it, but somehow she struggled through the rest of the week. Having her students and lessons to focus on helped. The kids were all so endearing, and little Emma carried right along just as chipper as always, in her own timid way. She didn't appear troubled by her impending move in the least. On the contrary, she seemed very excited about it. Her Aunt Jenny had offered to teach her how to milk the cows next door, and she was going to fill a special role in testing out new flavors of ice cream.

The more the little girl prattled on about the farm, the more Mary Ellen began to envision Misty Meadows in her mind's eye. It sounded like a fabulous place. Historic yet homey, with a huge stone hearth and broad oak floors. Large windows overlooked the pasture and there was a covered front porch with a tin roof that pinged a little song in the rain. At least that was how Emma described it. Mary Ellen was almost sad she couldn't see it for herself.

She was packing up her bags for the weekend when Wes rapped at her classroom door. "You know,

Thanksgiving is next Thursday..." he began tentatively. "And I was wondering what your plans are for the holiday?"

Mary Ellen had thought about going to DC, particularly since Liz had booked herself a December cruise so wouldn't be around at Christmas. Then, ultimately, she'd decided it was too long a drive for such a short time, and that she couldn't really afford the gas money. Mary Ellen also wasn't certain she was ready to face Liz again, so Liz could tell her everything that was wrong with her life.

Especially now that she was feeling down about things, Mary Ellen didn't want her mom's interference, or her insinuations that teaching and Mary Ellen were such a bad fit. Because, in spite of everything else, Mary Ellen didn't agree. She was a good teacher and she knew it. This wasn't just a profession, it was her calling. Being an educator was what Mary Ellen was meant to do.

"I'm going to be sticking around here," she admitted shyly, before giving a small shrug. "I suppose I'll stay home and fix something simple." She gazed at Wes tellingly. "I doubt I'll be cooking a turkey."

"Emma and I are planning on ham," Wes said decidedly. "At my folks' house. You're invited to join us."

She gasped in surprise.

"If you'll come."

Mary Ellen's pulse raced and her face burned hot. "I'd...er...that would be great!" After a moment, she managed to collect herself. "What can I bring?"

"Would you mind making a dessert?"

"Pumpkin pie or pecan?" Mary Ellen asked with a grin.

Chapter Fourteen

WES AND EMMA arrived at Mary Ellen's door around ten thirty on Thanksgiving morning. Wes had said he wanted to take Mary Ellen on a short drive on the way to his parents' house, and she'd agreed, thinking she'd enjoy spending the extra time with Wes and Emma. She still badly missed Crazy, though, and had encountered absolutely no luck in locating him.

Mary Ellen wished that she could be sure he'd been taken to a loving home, but it had sounded to her like the rooster had been adopted as a work animal. Not that this was necessarily a bad thing. All creatures needed their particular jobs to do, and perhaps Crazy had found his. Mary Ellen still hadn't decided what to do about the rooster coop in her yard. She supposed she'd have to disassemble it eventually.

"I'm sorry about Crazy," Emma said, her expression downcast. "Daddy told me last night that he moved away. To a different home."

"That's right, honey. I'm sorry, too," Mary Ellen said sadly. "I know we'll all miss him."

"Maybe he'll come see us?" Emma offered hopefully. "You know, for a visit?"

"He very well might," Mary Ellen said, trying to reassure the child. Though, in her heart, she knew it was no use. Crazy was long gone by now, and who knew where his new adoptive owner had taken him.

"Better grab your jacket," Wes advised. "It's extra nippy out this morning." Mary Ellen saw that, beyond him, the sky was bright blue, but the wind was brisk as it rippled through the trees. Most had lost their leaves by now, including the red maples towering near the edge of the cul-de-sac at the place where it abutted some farmland.

"And your hat and mittens, too!" Emma chimed in.

Mary Ellen grinned and grabbed her things off the coatrack. "Thanks so much for including me. I've been really looking forward to this day."

Wes shot her a warm smile. "So have we."

***

They crossed the cul-de-sac to the Johnsons' driveway and Wes opened the passenger-side door for Mary Ellen. As he did, she noted a stunning difference on his left hand. Wes was no longer wearing his wedding band. "Hop in," he said. "It will just take me a second to buckle Emma into her car seat."

Mary Ellen complied, her heart thudding wildly. Wes removing his ring had to mean something. Could she dare to hope the gesture had something to do with her? While her insides were bursting with excitement, Mary Ellen attempted to play it cool. "Where are we off to this morning?" she asked, buckling her seat belt.

"Emma and I were thinking you might like to see Misty Meadows," Wes said from behind her as he snapped Emma in.

"Your parents' place?" Mary Ellen asked over her shoulder.

"It's going to be my place now," Wes said contentedly. "I'm purchasing it properly from my mom and dad. We'll be transferring the deed in mid-December."

"How cool!" Mary Ellen peered at Emma. "You'll have a new home for Christmas."

"Uh-huh!" she answered happily. "And a super big Christmas tree!"

Mary Ellen smiled at the girl. "That sounds amazing."

Wes finished with Emma and climbed into the driver's seat, shutting his door. "Will you help us decorate it?"

Heat flooded Mary Ellen's cheeks. "Well, I..."

"It will be an awfully big job for just two people," Wes explained.

"Oh, right! Yes, of course. I'd love to help out. Sounds like fun."

"We're going to cut it down ourselves," Emma said. "There are lots of Christmas trees around the farm."

"I can't wait to see it," Mary Ellen answered as her heart hammered harder. Was Wes hinting at what she thought he was? That he wanted to continue spending personal time with her, after he and Emma had moved away from Sweetheart Valley Hills?

Wes smiled fondly. "I'm hoping you'll like it just as much as Emma and I do."

Mary Ellen couldn't imagine liking anything more than she enjoyed being around Wes and Emma. She was so pleased that Wes had invited her to spend Thanksgiving with his family. She'd called her mom this morning to wish her a happy holiday and had finally had it out with her. When Liz started in on Mary Ellen's "mistake" in moving to Paradise, Mary Ellen had told her that actually things were working out beautifully. Much better than expected...

She adored her job and she was good at it. She finally understood that teaching was what she was meant to do. Because she'd learned to own her life, other things were falling into place, as well. She wouldn't say exactly what, in part because Mary Ellen didn't completely know, but she assured her mom of one thing. Despite her unfortunate episode with losing Crazy, she was truly happy here in so many ways. When she said she hoped that Liz could be happy for her, Liz had stammered and said, "Well, it appears that Paradise has changed you."

"No, Mom," Mary Ellen answered. "The change was inside me all along."

They'd ended the call saying they loved each other, and with Liz making plans to visit Mary Ellen after the New Year. She promised not to pester Mary Ellen regarding her choices, and even said she'd be okay with Mary Ellen getting another rooster as a pet one day. Though Mary Ellen tried to assure Liz that was unlikely to happen anytime soon. Particularly with Calista Cartwright living nearby.

Mary Ellen leaned back in her seat, feeling newly empowered. She was proud of herself for confronting her mom, mostly because she'd done so in a mature and loving way. Mary Ellen had a new sense of self and felt a joyful anticipation about what the future might bring. For now, though, she was content to savor the scenic ride and the company of her two favorite people. The day was just beginning, and already it was turning out to be an awesome holiday.

***

They drove for several miles out into the countryside, passing various turn-offs to private farms situated behind rolling hills and sunny fields. The splendor of autumn was everywhere, with golds, reds, and oranges dotting the landscape with bold splashes of color like brushstrokes on an oil painting. "It's beautiful out here," Mary Ellen commented. "I haven't ventured this far outside of Paradise before."

"We're not really going that much farther beyond the school," Wes told her. "Turtle Creek Elementary is only a twenty minute drive from Misty Meadows."

"That's not much more of a drive than from Sweetheart Valley Hills."

"I know," Wes replied with a handsome grin. He flicked on his turn signal and soon they were traveling down a winding gravel road flanked by tall oaks, hickory and poplar trees.

"We're here!" Emma proclaimed, kicking her feet excitedly.

"The Smith Dairy is right next door," Wes offered happily.

"That's the one that belongs to your sister and her husband, Ian?"

"Yeah. Ian pretty much runs that business, while Jenny oversees the ice cream shop. She keeps threatening to cut back on her hours to start a family, but it hasn't happened yet."

"Do you think they're trying?" Mary Ellen inquired, intrigued.

Wes shrugged. "Maybe. But, as her big brother, I'm not asking. I figure Jenny will tell me when there's news to share."

"That would be fun for Emma," Mary Ellen said softly. "Having a little cousin around."

"Yes." Wes sent her a thoughtful glance before announcing, "Welcome to Misty Meadows!"

Mary Ellen stared out the windshield overwhelmed by the historic beauty of the farm. The old farmhouse was every bit as homey and inviting as she'd imagined. Only, it was tons bigger than she'd thought, with two full stories and a large front porch and a tall brick chimney on either side. "Wow!" she said, amazed. "How many fireplaces does the house have?"

"Four," Wes answered, putting his SUV in park.

"Are they all working?"

He turned to her and his green eyes sparkled. "They will be when I get done with them."

"What a fantastic old house," Mary Ellen said, taking it in again.

"It's got four bedrooms and three full baths," Wes told her. "The fireplaces are in the living room, two upstairs bedrooms, and in the downstairs master suite. I wish I could show you the inside, but there are renters living here until the end of the month."

Mary Ellen glanced around, not seeing any other vehicles parked in the circular drive in front of the fabulous farmhouse. There were a few outbuildings set a ways behind it, including what looked like a tool shed, a garage, and a small stable.

"They're away for Thanksgiving weekend," he explained in response to Mary Ellen's unasked query. "It's fine for us to look around the property, but obviously we can't go inside."

"No, no. That's fine," Mary Ellen said, still catching her breath over the gorgeous scenery. There was a wooden picket fence on the far side of the house. Way beyond that, she saw more mountains and what looked like a large barn.

"That's Ian and Jenny's place over there," Wes told her.

"How great!" Mary Ellen responded. "Jenny will be so close."

"Their farmhouse is on the other side of the big barn. It's not neighborhood-close, but it's not a bad hike, either. Not more than five miles away." He smiled pleasantly. "Want to get out and walk around?"

"Sure! I'd love that."

***

The moment Wes set Emma's little boots on the ground she took off running and squealing through the wind. She had her arms out beside her in her puffy purple coat and was flapping them, almost like she was a bird about to take flight.

"She seems so happy here," Mary Ellen commented to Wes as they stood by the fence.

Wes viewed his daughter wistfully. "I remember what that was like. To really run free."

"This must have been a wonderful place to grow up."

He met her eyes and Mary Ellen's heart skipped a beat.

"Daddy, Daddy!" Emma cried, racing toward them. "Can I go down to the creek?"

"Only if you don't go in it," Wes replied, chuckling.

Emma squealed and took off in that direction, shouting, "Yippee!" She only paused briefly to pick up a long stick and convert it into her pretend fairy princess wand. "I'm the Unicorn Princess!" she shouted, skipping merrily down the hill.

"Will she be all right?" Mary Ellen asked worriedly.

"Oh, yeah. The creek isn't much of a creek. Just a few inches of water tumbling over a path of smooth pebbles. Emma and I used to pick flowers along its banks in the spring."

"I'll bet your parents are happy about you moving here. You said at one time they considered selling Misty Meadows?"

"They could never bring themselves to do it."

"Why not, do you think?"

"I suppose they were waiting on me." He held her gaze for a prolonged beat. "Mary Ellen, I have a confession to make, and I hope you'll take it in the spirit that it's intended."

She anxiously surveyed his face, fearing something was wrong.

"It's not a bad thing," he said, apparently reading her expression. "I mean, at least I certainly don't want you to take it that way." He seemed really nervous about something. "It's just that I... I mean, this past Monday, I went in..." He paused and raked a hand through his hair.

"Went in where, Wes?"

"To Central Office. I needed to get something straight, and couldn't afford to take chances..."

"About...?"

"Us."

She watched Wes expectantly as he continued.

"I know this sounds crazy—oh man." He gave a pained laugh. "But I wanted to be sure to do the right thing. By you and by me, and of course by Emma... I didn't want either of us to compromise our jobs, or..." He exhaled deeply. "What I'm trying to tell you, Mary Ellen, is that I met with someone in the county personnel department: their educational ethics officer, and she said that just as long as you and I... I mean, if it's mutual. And we keep any sort of personal relationship completely out of school—"

Mary Ellen's heart pounded as she absorbed Wes's words. He'd gone to great lengths to be considerate and careful. Because Wes *was* interested... He wanted a relationship with her: a personal, romantic one. Wasn't that what he was saying? Her spirit soared when she realized that her insanely uncontrollable attraction to Wes hadn't been one-sided. He'd felt it every bit as ardently as she had. "I can't believe you went to all that trouble."

"I'd do it again." He leveled her a longing look. "In a heartbeat, if I knew that it would make a difference. And, make you feel more interested—"

"I *am* interested, Wes."

His brow rose with happy surprise.

"The truth is I don't believe I could *be* any more interested than this."

He viewed her tenderly. "Mary Ellen, you've got to know that I find you special."

Her pulse quickened and her face felt warm. "I think you're special, too. You and Emma, both. She's an incredible little girl."

"Thanks. I think so, too. Only..." He hesitated a moment then said softly, "I sometimes get the notion she's lonely."

"Lonely?"

"Emma did ask if you'd be her sister." Wes quirked a grin and Mary Ellen's heart stilled. "*Or* her mommy."

"Wes, I..."

"Although, truthfully, if I had another daughter, I'd probably rather start with an infant." He shared a playful look. "No offense."

"No... None taken." Mary Ellen's heart was beating so hard she would have sworn it was about to pound right through her chest.

"Look," he said gently, turning toward her. "I know that this isn't ideal, what with me being your boss and you being my teacher. But, I was wondering...if you think that someday in the future we might have a chance?"

"Wes Johnson," she said warmly. "Just what are you asking me?"

His Adam's apple rose and fell, then he pressed ahead. "I'm asking if you'd like to go out on a date with me. A real date, just the two of us. Because the truth is..." He swallowed hard before continuing. "Emma's not the only one who gets lonely. Sometimes I get lonely, too. But not just for anybody. For someone in particular. Mary Ellen," he said, gazing into her eyes. "I get lonely for you. When I'm not with you, when I don't see you, when I don't hear you singing at school down the hall..."

Mary Ellen cupped her hand to her mouth. "Oh, *gosh*."

"I love the sound of your voice." Wes grinned. "The plain truth is, it's pretty easy to love everything about you."

She gazed up at him with affection in her eyes and hope in her heart. "You're no slouch as a principal either, or as a dad and a neighbor. I imagine you'd make a pretty fine boyfriend, too."

A pleased expression crossed his face. "Boyfriend?"

"Well since you've already cleared things with Central Office..." She grinned saucily.

Just then, Emma came racing up the hill. "Daddy! Daddy! Miss Meeks! Look who I found!"

Mary Ellen could scarcely believe her eyes. Emma cradled a big, fat rooster in her arms, and that rooster appeared to be...Crazy!

"It can't be," she said with a gasp.

"Well, I'll be!" Wes set his hands on his hips and shook his head. "If that doesn't look like your rooster, it must be his double."

"It is Crazy!" Emma glowed as she scurried toward them. "I found him down by the creek digging up worms!" The little girl set down the bird, and he paraded across the grass and straight up to Mary Ellen.

"Crazy?" she said in stunned awe. "Is that really you?"

The big bird looked up at her with large dark eyes and blinked. Mary Ellen brought her hands to her mouth as tears sprang to her eyes. "It is Crazy! It's him!" She picked up the rooster and snuggled him against her, and Crazy let out a soft coo.

"He must have come from Jenny's farm," Wes said. "I can't think of any other explanation."

"Do you think she and Ian are the farmers who took him in?"

Wes grinned broadly. "I'm betting the answer is yes."

Mary Ellen hugged her long-lost pet tightly. "What are we going to do?"

"For now?" Wes said. "I think we should return him to the Smith Dairy. But, if I know my sister—and I'm sure I do—I'm certain we'll be able to work out a different sort of arrangement for the future."

"Can we move Crazy's coop?" Emma petitioned. "And his sign?"

Wes glanced Mary Ellen's way. "Only if that's okay with Miss Meeks."

"Whatever is best for Crazy is best for me," Mary Ellen said sincerely.

"Then, let's take Crazy back to the SUV," he said to Emma. "And drop him off at Aunt Jenny's. I can talk to her more about particulars over Thanksgiving dinner."

Crazy wriggled in Mary Ellen's arms and she whispered to the bird, "Don't worry, we're having ham."

Wes chuckled and Emma giggled.

"Can I carry him to the SUV?" the little girl asked sweetly.

Mary Ellen glanced at Wes for his approval. When he nodded, she said, "Sure," carefully transferring the rooster into Emma's small arms.

"Come on, Crazy," Emma said, striding in front of them. "It's time to go home."

"Yeah," said Wes, gazing longingly at Mary Ellen. "It's time to go home." He held out his hand and said warmly, "What do you say? Are you coming with us?"

Mary Ellen laid her hand in his and her heart fluttered. "Yes," she said, smiling up at him.

Wes smiled back. "Talk about a *crazy* way to meet the girl of your dreams."

With her free hand, Mary Ellen play-punched him. "Maybe that old rooster knew something we didn't?"

Wes laughed then eyed her thoughtfully.

"I think you're going to like my folks."

"I'm sure I'll love them."

"They're definitely going to love you."

"Wes?"

"Huh?" he asked, as they followed along behind Emma.

Mary Ellen smiled brightly, sunny warmth radiating through her soul. "Happy Thanksgiving."

"Happy Thanksgiving to you." His green eyes sparkled, then he gave her a light kiss. "I can't wait to say merry Christmas."

The End

Author Bio

NEW YORK TIMES and *USA Today* bestselling author
Ginny Baird has published novels in print and online
and received screenplay options from Hollywood for
her family and romantic comedy scripts. Whether
writing lighthearted romantic comedy or spine-tingling
romantic suspense, she delights in delivering
heartwarming stories. Ginny is the author of the
Christmas Town series, the Holiday Brides series, the
Summer Grooms series, a Romantic Ghost Stories
series, and several standalone books. She invites you to
visit her website and connect with her on social media.
http://www.ginnybairdromance.com